UNCLE TOM'S GABBIN'
& SO AM I

An anthology from

Uncle Thomas Sullivan
and
Niece Catherine Astolfo

CARRICK
PUBLISHING

Uncle Tom's Gabbin' & So Am I

An anthology from Uncle Thomas Sullivan and Niece
Catherine Astolfo

Copyright © 2013 Catherine Astolfo and

Thomas Sullivan

Astolfo, Catherine, 1950—
Sullivan, Thomas, 1933—

Print Edition 978-1-927114-75-9

Photograph on cover by Vincent Astolfo

Cover Design by Sara Carrick

Carrick Publishing
3901 Don Mills Road, # 47
Toronto, ON M2H 2S7
www.carrickpublishing.com
carrickpublishing@rogers.com

Table of Contents

My First Romance

(OR: Surviving the lies of tainted love, untarnished by reality)

By Tom Sullivan

It has been said that your first love is your only true love. I'm not sure that this is true but sometimes I just like to believe it. My first love was Patsy Thompson. In late 1940's Tupperton, sex and love were not synonyms, at least not to a pre-teen boy. The real problem with my love for Patsy was that everyone else, including both girls and boys, in our grade eight class at McHugh Public School, loved Patsy too.

A pre-class gathering in the school hall? Patsy was at the center both physically and socially. If Patsy were present, attention was received and dispensed in equal measure. She had a manner that included interest in even the marginalized. Although I was convinced that Patsy was particularly sweet to me, she was actually the same with all others. I loved talking to her, yet knew she never looked on me as anything more than just another classmate. Hopalong Cassidy never told a girl he loved her and neither would I. Love unverbalized but not undreamt.

I'd fantasize that she and I were out on one of the ferry rides in the lake and somehow the boat sank and she and I were the only ones who survived and we had to grow up together and eat coconuts and berries but we liked each other and had a great time doing it. It didn't matter that the ferryboats that ran out of Toronto Harbour were never more than a mile or so from shore and that there were no islands let alone ones where coconuts would grow in the cold Canadian winter. If I could imagine Patsy being in love with me I could certainly deal with Canadian coconuts.

Patricia Louisa Thompson spoke fluent Spanish. Her parents lived in Ecuador but during the school year she stayed with her aunt and uncle in Tupperton. Patsy was an enigma. She never seemed to be hiding her past, but she never spoke of it either. She looked Spanish, but how could one reconcile this with the name "Thompson"? And she spoke perfect English without even a trace of accent. But she did disappear each June at the end of the school term and showed up again in the fall saying only that she spent the summer in Ecuador. Some of her girlfriends said that they got postcards from her with an Ecuador stamp, legitimizing the story.

Patsy's aunt and uncle owned and operated the oldest funeral home in Tupperton. It was a huge hundred year-old brick house that was obviously once the home of early wealthy Tupperton merchants. The house had a veranda that ran its whole length and was supported by large ornate white pillars that were carved with circles and flowers. Three large circular turrets and gabled windows graced the front along with a large circular driveway which could accommodate four or even five cars, with room remaining for a large hearse.

Patsy claimed that she slept on the third floor right next to where they made up the corpses for show. We asked if there were ever corpses in there while she was in bed in the next room. She looked quite surprised and said that yes, of course there were, almost all the time. This spooked the hell out of the rest of us, but Patsy treated it as though it were the most normal situation imaginable.

Patsy was far and away the prettiest girl in our class. She had bright green eyes and an olive skin that seemed to have a slight glow. Her teeth were exceptionally white and she smiled often. She had long dark hair that was obviously wavy but always worn in pigtails. Patsy was pretty, but when she came back to school in the fall of our grade eight year, she was absolutely beautiful.

One week, my daydream nearly came true. I was supposed to go to the movies with Harold Smithey but his grandmother said that he had a slight fever and had to stay home that day. I decided to go alone. I got into the movie house a little late and had to find my way to my seat in the dark. To my astonishment, I sat just two seats away from Patsy. She waved and I moved over and sat beside her. Big step.

Her little cousin Henry, who was about five, sat on the other side of her. The cartoons ended and the main show started. I stared hard at the screen but I never saw what was on. I was thinking hard about sliding my hand over and holding Patsy's hand. The boys in my class would talk about girls but I don't think any of us really did much about it, so I wasn't sure what to do.

My mouth went sort of dry. My hands started to sweat, so I wiped my left hand on my pants and put it on the armrest. I dangled it so that my fingertips just barely touched the back of her hand, which was on her knee. To my surprise and delight, Patsy turned her hand over, took a firm grip and placed our clenched hands together on her lap. I was in ecstasy! I thought that this might mean we were boyfriend and girlfriend and that I might even kiss her sometime.

I was dreaming about this and still had no idea of what was happening on the screen when Patsy suddenly let go of my hand and whispered: "I got to go to the washroom" and she got up and left. I noticed that my hand had started to sweat again. I wiped it off on my pants and hung it over the seat in front with my fingers spread open so that the air could get in and my hand wouldn't be all sweaty when she came back.

I was all excited. I planned to grab her hand as soon as she sat down and maybe even interlock our fingers and put our hands in my lap and God knows where that might lead. Canadian coconuts didn't seem quite so ridiculous. Would I put my arm around her shoulder? No, that would have to wait for another time. I didn't want to rush things. When she came back I'd play it cool.

Her absence lasted through an ambush and a barroom brawl. I thought she might be looking for her seat so I stood up.

Henry, the little cousin, who didn't even seem to notice that Patsy had left, said, "Hey, where are you going?"

I sat down quickly. Henry moved into the seat beside me that had been deserted by Patsy. Henry had the sniffles and no visible means of controlling or abating them. As good as he was at sniffling, he was much better at emitting gas and asking questions. He wanted to know why the man in the black hat had hit the young cowboy. I told him that it was because the young cowboy kept farting and Henry accepted this with a nod. He asked me several more questions.

A guy sitting behind said that if I can't keep the kid quiet, he was going to call the usher and have us both thrown out. I apologized. Henry had brought a comic book which I borrowed to wave frantically in the air in the hopes of creating a much diluted methane gas environment in anticipation of Patsy's return. This didn't please the fellow behind who moved to a more environmentally friendly part of the theatre.

At the end of the movie, Patsy had not returned to her seat. What was I going to do with this kid?

Just as the lights went on Patsy appeared at the end of the aisle. She said simply, "Sorry, I ran into Eileen Dixon. Come on, Henry." And without another word, she left the theater with Henry in tow.

I watched my only prepubescent love life disappear in the crowd up the aisle.

Hooked on Whales

(Hooked on Whales originally published in NorthWord Literary Magazine)

by Catherine Astolfo

The old man sits in his rocking chair, a quilt tucked over his legs. Eyes focused on a point somewhere beyond the window, his paper hands flutter very slightly. A long black car pulls up in front of the house. Three people alight, walk in a straight line up the sidewalk to the entranceway, and open the screen door confidently. The old man does not turn.

They are familiar with the place. Busily they kiss cheeks, shake hands. The younger man and his wife perch on the stiff visitors' chairs. They say cheerful things as they sip tea. Others in the room respond with the kind of polite chitchat that strangers often share. The old man does not take part in the conversation. They do not expect anything from him, so the words flow around and past him. He notices that the boy does not participate either. Instead, the youngster sits and holds the old man's trembling hand.

He thinks of the sea, the way it calls to him.

It's the most easterly point in North America, his Da told them - stand here with your back to the sea and the entire population of the continent is west of you. At the shore, the wind whipped them with pleasant salty warmth. His Da motioned for the children to open their presents now. The boys unfurled their lines. The kites bobbed in the wind, blue and red against the sun. For a long time the boy and his brothers watched the breezes catch the little diamonds of cloth and whip them around next to the clouds.

The woman sits close to him, calls his name from time to time, speaks of the weather, of times past. He is aware that she is related to him, to the boy at his side, but she is not blood. Classic responses to her chatter fade on his lips.

The old man remembers what it was like to feel the water below the boat, to have the wind lash his face with salt. Instead of the screen surrounding the porch he sees the evergreens etching the sky, the stars falling to the sea. He feels an ache of remembrance.

Up and up he climbed the steps toward the lighthouse. Buttercups and purple irises lined the pathway. Now he was above the beach and could look out from the other side of the harbour. Suddenly he saw a puff of water and up came the whales, their backs glistening in the sun. The wind howled. White waves crashed against the shore. He stood for a very long time, just staring at the ocean, its fierce beauty laid out before him. He fell in love. He was hooked on whales.

The younger man gets up and straightens the cover lying over the rocking chair. This one is related by blood, the old man thinks. Son? Yes, perhaps. Yawning and stretching, the son walks to the screen. The old man watches him through veiled eyes.

Something the woman says causes the man at the screen to laugh. The sound is cold and forced, unnatural. Not a gusty laugh like the old man remembers from his colleagues on the sea. This man is cultured beyond true joy. Son? Did this son call him Da, the way he referred to his own father so long ago?

The youngster begins to speak, still sitting there beside the rocking chair, keeping the unruly hand from quivering. Although the old man does not catch the words, he feels the focus in the room shift to the boy. The Son and the related woman stiffen, faces taut with anger. There is ice in the man's voice as he tells the boy to mind his own business, reminds him that Granddad just might be able to hear him.

The old man turns his gaze to see the boy better. Long thin hands are clasped in the young man's lap. His eyes are bold. There are more words, angry, defiant from the child, defensive and shocked from the Son.

The boy crouches in front of the rocking chair. His countenance is profound and strong. Grandson. Son of the Son, but so different. Watching carefully, the old man sees the words on his grandson's lips, feels the roughness in the boyish hands.

"I would take you out in the Maria, Granddad. We could stay on one of the islands until it was your time. Not in this old home." The way he says home resonates, drags the old man to the surface, then plunges him back to the past.

The rocky cliffs ringed the roads. The trees were an old green fence, bent in the direction of the wind. The sun was warm and the wind refreshing, but as he headed out to sea, the waves were high. The Maria plowed up and then down again, a swing and a dip.

Suddenly the whale was there, a huge male Humpback, friendly as all get-out, showing off. His tail lifted up and out, over and over, glinting white and silver, sometimes slipping gracefully under the waves, sometimes slapping a loud tattoo. Proud and joyful, the animal came right up to the ship. Tail up, down, sprays of white foam. Rolled over. Fins in the air, first one, then two, then one again. This time he slapped the surface with his fin and the sound reverberated throughout the bay. He dove and came back up, puffing spray right beside the Maria, so close they could've touched him.

Straightening, the boy follows the Son's command that he leave. The screen door slams very loudly. Grandson.

The old man smiles. He remembers steering the boat in the rain, pushing her against the current and the waves, driving for the light on the shore. You had to have courage. You had to defy everything.

Incredulous, almost frightened, the woman's voice sounds loud in his ear. "Arthur—your dad's smiling!"

The man sits down again. "Dad. It's Arthur, your son."

Soft hands reach to stroke the old ones. Son. He thinks of his own Da, the set of his shoulders, the sun creases over his face, the fat thick fingers. He remembers how rough and blue his own hands would be after a day on the sea. So strong he could crack a nut. Or hold the wheel of a ship in driving hail. This Son is weak, hesitant, simpering.

A flicker of regret washes over him. He remembers all at once that this Son was half an orphan. He, the Father, was never home. Unlike his own Da, he never took the Son out on the boat, never shared his love of the ocean. Never bought him a kite or took him to Cape Spear. Kept him from the joy and the addiction.

He feels the water smacking against the bottom of the boat, sees the warm glow of the fire on the shore. The damp. The salt. The search.

His blue and white boat waited for them, sitting flat on the sea. Mist hovered halfway up the hillsides; birds circled overhead. The inlet remained calm, barely rippling. Small lines of current drifted in now and then. All they heard was the hum of his boat and the call of the sea gulls.

The sky was still a light grey, covered in mist, clouds touching their heads and the mast of the ship. Fog sat across the evergreens like a delicate mummer's veil. The rocks added to the impossible beauty because they were every different hue and line. Slate smeared through a hill of granite. Purple-tinged, yellow, orange, white and black, the stones and rocks were, of course, what gave Newfoundland its nickname: The Rock. As soon as the mist cleared, they chugged out to the open sea. The search had begun.

The silence in the room is uncomfortable. The woman begins her bright chatter again as someone comes to replenish the tea-things, offers him a steaming cup. He does not reply. He sees the Atlantic lapping at his ship, rocking her gently.

On the first leg of the journey, he spied some Minke whales cavorting in the bay. The tourists were a friendly, pleasant bunch, excited and thrilled, despite the worsening weather. When a slanting cold rain began pelting them, they simply pulled up the hoods of their suits. He didn't often find a group such as these: the ones who loved the land and the sea almost as much as he. He took them into the bay, where the local fellas took their girlfriends and mothers to make a good first impression. He pointed out the huge adult bald eagle, huddled against the rock, nearly invisible. Suddenly the bird took wing, spreading his beautiful feathers into the rain cloud, flapping above their heads for a moment before he circled off into the distance. This is a sign to good luck, he told the group.

At first, the old man doesn't respond to his son's touch. Not because he doesn't want to, but because he cannot. The Son has no idea what this prison is like, he thinks. And that idiot wife of his – well, she performs this once a week obligatory clinking of teacups, inane conversation. Does she think he is of no use now? Is she politely waiting, waiting, for him to draw his last breath? He remembers the catch of sea salt in his throat when he breathed in the ocean air.

Just as the boat reached the mouth of the bay, there they were: two of them—Fin whales. They were prettier than the Humpback, with lovely smooth black and white skin and a thick, sturdy Fin. He told the tourists that fin whales were "hard workers", less showy than the Humpback, but also a less common sight. This was the luck our eagle drew us to, he said.

There were two of them, feeding on capelin along the shore. He steered the boat to follow them at a respectful distance as they dipped below, grazed, and came puffing to the surface. The whales chased the capelin into shore by flashing their white bellies. The fish raced toward the shore, where they were suddenly swallowed up by a giant mouth. He loved the look on the tourists' faces when he informed them that Fin whales were so big they could swallow this zodiac in one gulp. Second biggest animal in the world.

Once the fin whales were satiated, they dove beneath the surface. The tourists were disappointed, though he could see a flat oval of water where the whales might still be.

Suddenly, there she was: about ten feet away, her enormous body dwarfing his not-so-little boat. She surfaced and puffed, as though in greeting. He was silent in amazement and reverence for this gorgeous, gentle animal, just as the tourists were struck dumb with awe. This whale could indeed swallow them, but she came to play instead.

The Son is preparing to leave now, as he gently returns the ancient hand to its lap. The old man takes a shuddering breath, squeezes his muscles with great effort. He feels as though he is lifting an enormous weight, a dead useless thing. But it is only his arm, with its trembling leafy hand, scarred and blue lined, calluses faint memories on white skin. He places his hand on this Son's soft one. An offering, an apology.

I was addicted, he wants to say, I am sorry I was no Da. I was hooked on whales, not on life, not you, not your mother. I found a job that fed my addiction. I spent far more time with tourists and the Maria than I did with you. But he has no words, no way to force these thoughts from his head to his tongue. He smiles again, though he knows his mouth must look twisted and awkward.

The Son looks happy, though. He clings to the dead leaf as though it is a gift. The woman fetches the young boy, who once again squats in front of the chair. The old man keeps the muscles taut, forcing the smile, until a grey haze begins to fill him up. There are tears in the eyes of both these younger males. The old man briefly wonders why. Then he wonders who they are.

Later, in the dusk of the waning day, he awakens. Somewhere in the recess of his mind, he recalls something momentous. A good feeling, a kind of warmth, spreads through his limbs and he thinks there has been a leap forward. Perhaps the Humpback has come back to play. Perhaps the Fins have resurfaced. He decides to go for a walk.

Shawl over his shoulders, he begins to move up the deserted street. Already he can hear the roar of the surf against the shore.

When he is there, he stands for a long time in the wind, listening. It is grey, moody. It would take a strong man to handle the sea today. Perhaps a man such as his grandson would some day grow into.

He thinks of the walls at the home, of the screen porch, of the rocking chair. Dreams that he is back there again.

Shivering, he gets up and walks toward the water.

From the other side, they heard the sound of her mate, poof, a powerful spurt of water signaling his arrival. You are so fortunate, he told the Fin-whale tourists. I've never seen them come this close. Say hello, they've come where you're to. The group stood in place, mouths open, a look of gratitude on their faces. A look he never got tired of seeing. He never took the job for granted, considered it a gift instead. He was useful, a teacher. He was strong and brave and he was in love with the whales and the sea.

The water reaches out to touch him. He sinks his feet in it, then his hands, tastes the salt on his lips. Slowly he walks into the waves, feeling the ocean cold and clingy, yet welcoming. His eyes slide shut and he drifts, floating, peaceful. He lets the sea take him.

The rocking chair is still.

Home At Last

By Tom Sullivan

"Good morning Mr. Marne, welcome to our table," said Emilie Marks, the self-appointed chairwoman of the breakfast table.

Andy smiled, nodded as he looked from face to face around the table. "Please call me Andy," he said cheerfully.

"Oh, Andrew, what a nice name. We haven't had an Andrew since Andrew Weise. Andrew is no longer with us." Emilie kept a full-tooth smile, the like of which is rarely seen outside toothpaste ads.

"He died," Marveen said. Arthritis and enormous glasses precluded her looking up. Marveen was dressed in a long red dress with a dainty white scarf carefully and tastefully tucked in at the neck. Her huge red-rimmed glasses emphasized her narrow face. Age and arthritis had rounded her shoulders resulting in a direct line of sight that terminated at her breakfast plate. Conversational eye contact was difficult and painful, so she rarely attempted it. Meaning and message came in short emphatic statements. "He died," she repeated. "It's about the only way to leave here," she added casually.

Emilie gave an embarrassed smile. "Oh, Andrew, you'll find our table a spirited lot... full of fun and whimsy," she said. "Why don't you tell us a little bit about yourself, Andrew?"

In less than a minute Andy gave a number-biased scan of his life: Born in Toronto 1930, engineer 1954, same firm thirty-eight years, married fifty-seven years, widowed three, present age eighty-two. As he spoke, he looked around the table at the heads briefly nodding as though they had heard parallel tales a number of times. Or, more likely, have recounted similar tales not so long ago.

It was Andy's first day at Parallel Pines Lodge, known locally as the old age home or senior citizens residence depending chiefly on the age of the labeler. He had been married to not-quite his childhood sweetheart, Louellen Garrott for fifty-seven tiny years and they had been inseparable. In private intimate moments... the only ones he still remembered clearly, he had called her Lou-lee and she replied in a sing-song fashion, as though they were exchanging mating calls.

The decision to move to Parallel Pines, or PP as the night nursing staff called it with a soft chuckle, was not made easily or quickly. The argument for the move was all accurate: forgetting medication, cooking meals, empty house (apartment actually), unhealthy heart. All sound reasons for the move. The only argument against: Andy really didn't like old people very much.

His children were gentle but persuasive: "You'll love it there, Dad. They have pool, darts, a library, social nights. And the food is all prepared for you. No worries."

The unmentioned reasons included his bad heart and the relief they would feel knowing someone else was seeing to his needs. His three children loved him... or had loved and even envied the parental package of which he was an important but subordinate part. He had no doubt of that. But they had jobs and children and responsibilities and all the practical side of life to cater to... they did not need the burden... loved as it was.

Andy had arrived at the lodge mid-evening and was shown directly to his room. He had been at an orientation session the previous weekend and felt fairly familiar with the lodge. The room was quite tastefully appointed, neutrality being the operative word, really. The bed was three-quarters... too large for one but too small for company... as if he needed reminding. There was a larger than expected color TV, assuaging filial guilt, and a small fridge empty except for a pint of milk and a package of whole wheat biscuits. A small box of tea bags and a tin of instant coffee sat on the counter right next to the kettle. A very comfortable leather armchair faced a small round table and a visitors' chair that was severe enough to discourage prolonged occupancy. The large bay window looked out onto a near-vacant parking lot, which was hemmed by an attractive grove of trees. City lights blinked in the distance.

The buffet breakfast was scheduled for eight o'clock and all were expected to be at their assigned tables by then. This served as an attendance check and, if there were any absentees, their rooms were checked by staff in the hope that no one had gone astray. Passed away in the night was quite acceptable. Strayed away was not.

With the exception of a winter holiday in Florida where he shared a bedroom with two grandchildren, this was the first time since his wife's death that he slept in a room that he had not shared with her. It was strangely painful. It was Saturday. Every Saturday morning for about forty years he and his wife followed a silly (was silly, now sad) routine whereby he would "butle" her. She would sit up in bed and he would bring her coffee, with sliced tomatoes on toast on a tray with the Saturday edition of the newspaper. For added effect, he would serve this on the best silverware tray in his best headwaiter tradition; he would then bow and ask, "Will there be anything else, madam?"

He would then sing a truncated version of "Have I Told You lately That I Love You." They would then both laugh, only partly at his singing efforts. The ritual had always seemed cute... now to him it seemed golden. He slipped out of his clothes and got into bed immediately.

The breakfast table was occupied by four women and two men. Andy was told that this was pretty close to the sex ratio of the residents at the lodge.

"Oh, Andrew, you couldn't have arrived on a better day!" gushed Emilie... "Sunday... the Lord's day," spoken with all the pauses and emphasis that she could muster. "The Reverend Gorbhan Halliday will be here to lead us all in our march to salvation."

"I'm not a religious person," said Andy, far too meekly to deter Emilie.

"Neither was I, before I was led into the light. Oh, come just once and experience your own transformation. Eleven o'clock in the common room. Everybody will be there!" Andy looked around the table. George, his sole male comrade gave a slight shoulder shrug and a facial expression equivalent to "what the hell, I haven't anything else to do."

Laverne Possen sat to Emilie's right. Laverne was a small, unadorned woman with quick darting eyes and a constant expression of surprise. During the meal she asked "What time is it?" at least five times. She wore a long-sleeved blouse with puffed shoulders and an incongruent scarf. She ate her breakfast in a series of tiny morsels suspended on a fork.

Betty Bauncer seemed enthralled with every word Emilie said. She kept her eyes glued on her every time she spoke and looked around the table and nodded enthusiastically following every remark Emilie made. Betty looked surprisingly young to be in a seniors' home. Her hair was curly and assisted blonde and her smile seemed somehow sweet and genuine. Her face was relatively wrinkle-free.... with the emphasis on "relatively."

Andy arrived at the common room just before eleven o'clock. There were fewer people in the room than he had anticipated... perhaps twenty all told. The focus of the gathering was at the small table at the front and Andy could clearly see the head and shoulders of a tall slim gentleman too young to be a resident. Reverend Halliday, Andy correctly surmised. The half-dozen people encircling him were all female and all talking quietly at once while they each gathered a small number of pamphlets that had been placed on the table. Among those standing by the table was Emilie, her smile reflecting her anticipation and enthusiasm for the proceedings. Andy took a seat in the back row and noticed that George of the breakfast table was just a few seats away. As soon as George saw Andy he came and sat beside him, nodding but not saying a word.

The service lasted about three-quarters of an hour with the Reverend Halliday assuring everyone that the Lord loved and welcomed them all and would personally welcome each one as they went to join him in heaven.... Provided, of course, that each had accepted the Lord Jesus Christ as his/her personal savior. At the end of the reverend's assurances, the congregation were invited to sing "Come to me, oh Lord" found on page four of the pamphlet, while the three who were new to the group came forward and knelt while Reverend Halliday placed his right hand on each head and with left hand reaching upward, called upon the Lord to welcome the newcomer to his kingdom. Andy complied, although reluctantly. The meeting concluded and Andy made his way passed the large open jar with the sign encouraging donations in order to carry on the crusade for souls.

The next morning at breakfast, Emilie smiled so broadly that every other feature of her face was dismissed to a secondary role, if it had any role at all. When Andy entered, all were seated just as they had been the morning before and Emilie's greeting was even more effusive.

"Oh, there is the new soldier for the Lord," she cried as Andy took his seat. "Your soul must be soaring with new-found joy!"

Andy felt that he could not carry the deception, even though it was not his deception, any longer. "I really don't believe any of it," he said.

Silence followed and Emilie's smile retreated to the extent that her lips resembled a tiny volcanic mound. Wrinkles and gaping eyes dominated her face. "But I saw the joy on your face…"

Andy cut her off: "You saw what you wanted to see, Emilie. The truth is that I very deeply doubt that there is any personal God who cares about us now or in eternity. I would love to believe that my wife is "up there" waiting for me, but I don't." A long silence followed.

"You know, you're right. It's all horseshit," offered George. It was the longest sentence Andy had heard from George since he arrived at the lodge.

Marveen said: "It really is just our own way of thinking, isn't it? Nothing to it, really." She looked down as though someone had told her of a recent death.

Laverne asked for the time.

Emilie said, "Well, I will pray for you all and ask the Lord to bring you to your senses so that you won't all spend an eternity in hell. But the choice will be yours!" She emphasized the last sentence with a finger firmly planted on table.

Betty looked around the room and said, "Well, I don't know what to think."

"Think thoughts of the Lord and pray that you are not blinded to the truth by those who would do you evil." Emilie glared at Andy.

The rest of the meal went by in uneasy silence, except Laverne asked the time twice more.

That night Andy lay in bed reading a detective novel, when a faint knock came to his door. He put the book down, straightened his pajama top and went to the door. Much to his consternation, Emilie stood outside looking very grieved. "What is it you want Emilie?" he asked.

"Only a minute of your time, Andrew."

"Emilie, I'm very tired and it is almost eleven o'clock."

"Only two minutes, I promise. Don't harden your heart to my plea."

More than anything Andy opened the door hoping she would accept that not all non-believers had hardened hearts.

Emilie stepped in and breathed a sigh of relief. "Andrew, I respect your beliefs"... she did not. "Andrew I respect your right to hold your beliefs." She felt better with this.

Andy said, "But?"

Emilie began softly, almost conciliatory, but her language became more rushed while varying wildly in volume: sometimes soft and almost indistinguishable and then loud and threatening. Andy followed fragments;

"turning souls from the Lord" "eternal damnation" "agony and pain of hell."

In one brief pause Andy managed to say: "I'm not trying to convince anyone of anything. I just don't believe and I don't want to pretend that I do."

Emilie sobbed uncontrollably and suddenly grabbed Andy's pajama collar, one lapel in each hand and pulled his face so close to hers that their noses were almost touching. Emilie's eyes seemed to reflect the light from his bedside lamp and the tears magnified her pupils. False eyelashes…mascara… false, remnants of rouge and lipstick… all false. No person there at all.

Andy wanted to scream at her. "Get a life, become real!" But there was no "real", only desperation and terror and hate and no person. Andy felt anger rising in his chest. Emilie was now pulling so tightly on his lapels that he began to have a slight choking sensation. He could easily have punched her in the face to make her let go, but that just wasn't Andy. He grabbed both her wrists and pulled down as hard as he could. He gasped and became aware of a sharp pain in his lower left jaw that seemed to cause diminished vision in his left eye the pain shot down his left arm and seemed to try and escape through his chest. He knew. He was having a heart attack.

"Pills," he breathed out. "Pills," he said much more indistinctly.

Andy pulled himself away and staggered to his bedside table. He fumbled but managed to pick up the small bottle of heart tablets. His hand shook and he could not open it. He pushed it toward Emilie and slurred "Pilzz, op'n pillz."

Emilie took the bottle and glanced at the label.

"Pilzz ples!" repeated Andy.

Emilie looked at him in triumph. "Don't you see, Andrew? God cannot have you damning souls!"

Andy grabbed the bottle but his fingers would not work. He pushed the bottle toward Emilie and said softly, " Pilzz PLEES, pillz" As conscious faded, he recalled the love of his life and breathed, "Lo-lee, Lo-lee" and fell to the floor.

"Oh, Andrew, I heard you trying to call to the Lord! I'm sure you were heard. That's all you need for salvation. I'm so happy for you, Andrew."

She left his room, left him lying where God had placed him and went back to her own room, smiling.

The next morning when Andy did not show for breakfast, the staff checked his room and found him dead on the floor. His heart pills were nowhere to be found.

What Kelly Did*

(*Arthur Ellis Award winner for Best Crime Short Story in Canada, 2012, originally published in NorthWord Literary Magazine)

By Catherine Astolfo

He stands in the doorway, backlit by the yellow light from a dusty bulb. The Toronto Police Department seems to have emptied itself onto the street, all shoulders and legs and guns. It's 1976 and these scenes are still uncommon, so numerous city news reporters are here too, standing on the other side of the road, sprinters waiting for the starter pistol to explode.

When the policeman in charge asks me if I am the one they have summoned, I simply nod. They lead me toward the boy, surrounding me like a protective animal pack. I find breathing difficult. I am close enough now that I can see him. I am not sure that he can see me.

He is upright and stiff, his eyes glazed. Both arms cradle a rifle, a huge weapon that looks too heavy for someone so slight. Blood is spattered over his face and shirt. Bits of white and other reddish globs cling to his clothing and hair.

"Kelly?" I say, gently, a question because I am not sure he still resides inside his own body.

He turns those eyes to meet mine and the past washes into the present, an eight-year flood of memories, regrets and grief.

***

I found him on the steps of my portable classroom, curled up tight, his thin arms wrapped around his bony legs. He was fast asleep, a tattered little ball of dirty skin and ripped clothing. When I reached down to touch his shoulder, I could smell him, unwashed and pungent. He twitched when my fingers nudged against him and sat up, sending a puff of malodorous breath up my nostrils. His own nose was crusted with dried snot. He wiped his eyes against one sleeve and blinked at me. That's when it happened.

We connected.

He was beautiful, even from the depths of his abject need. His eyes were a deep blue that you usually only see in paintings of the ocean. Ringed with long black lashes, they were wide and startling in his thin face. Angular jaw, high cheekbones, he had a movie star's face with his pure little-boy skin. His hair was brown with sunny threads of blond; he wore it in a long, unruly mop that swept over his forehead.

As novice teachers, we were warned not to get too close to the children: keep yourself distanced, objective, don't touch them, don't like them too much. Above all, do not love them.

With the haughty prejudice of a white privileged woman-child, barely out of my teens, I was certain I'd never have that problem in this school. Depressed, violent, slum and crazy were all words that had been applied to the people and the area of Toronto where my first school was situated. I wasn't happy to be placed here, but I had not been given a choice. I wanted a job, I lived in the city, so I took the position. It'll only be for a year, Robin, everyone assured me. It will look great on your resume. You survive in that climate, you can teach anywhere.

But in that moment, when he tried to erase grief and sleeplessness from his eyes, I forgot everything I had learned. I forgot to be distant or objective. I forgot that I was not allowed to love or protect him.

"What's your name?" I asked him cheerfully, as though finding him asleep on the porch an hour before bell time was normal.

"Kelly," he answered, lowering his gaze from mine, jiggling his leg nervously.

"Hey, you're in my class," I said. I knew I had a Kelly on my list, an unusual name in this section of town. "Did you come to help me with the blackboards?"

He glanced up quickly to see if I was teasing, but I kept my eyes steady. He nodded, jumping to his feet in one bounce as only little boys can manage.

"Excellent. I was really hoping someone would come and help."

I stuck the key in the door and shoved it open. A blast of hot air shifted from inside to the cool air of the early morning, hitting us on the head as it whooshed outward. Decorating, planning, straightening, dusting and cleaning had all been accomplished by my own hand. Despite my ministrations, the classroom was mildewy and dilapidated; the floor stained by years of running shoes and ink. With no little bodies to fill up the space, our entry echoed. Our feet pounded across the tile. The little boy glanced guiltily away from the coat racks, as though it were a crime to have no knapsack to place there.

Kelly's face was alight with the comfort that comes out of the transition from goose bumps to sweat. He was suddenly active. Before I could stop him, he went straight to the ledge and began to wipe the boards. All of the careful printing I'd placed there became smudges of white up to the height of his outstretched arm.

I sighed but didn't let it travel across my tongue. Instead, I arranged papers, put a pencil and eraser on each desk.

"Miss?"

"Yes, Kelly?"

"That's as good as I can do it."

He glanced mournfully at the letters beyond his tiptoes.

"That's okay," I said. "How about if you give out the rulers?" I nodded toward a stack on my desk.

He meticulously distributed the straight pieces of wood, making sure each one was aligned perfectly with the pencil. I set about reapplying the lessons on the chalkboard. When we were both finished, I pulled cookies and apples from my briefcase.

"Let's sit and rest a bit before the other kids get here," I told him.

He gulped the first cookie in one bite, gnawed the apple down to its core, and then he ate mine.

***

He is still beautiful. His eyes are layered now, though, shadowed and haunted. He looks as if he has forgotten how to smile.

"Kelly," I repeat. "It's Miss Stewart. Remember?"

He shifts a subtle movement of the gun that has my wolf pack standing alert. I try to step forward, so he can see me apart from the group.

"What's happened here, Kell?"

He is very tall now, still thin and bony, his body a collection of angles and points. His face is long and his skin unblemished, even in adolescence. He looks insolent, wary, as though I am a stranger. I almost recoil from the glare he flings at me.

"You mean, what have I done?" he asks, his voice thick with sarcasm and the deep tones of a burgeoning manhood.

"That's not what I said," I answer. "I just want to know what happened. I want to know if you're hurt."

He briefly lowers his eyelashes to glimpse the blood and entrails glued to his shirt, but he maintains his stance in the doorway. The police cordon does not move.

"Yah, I guess that's one conclusion you could come to," he says. I am frightened by the undertone of laughter that tinges his words.

***

The other kids refused to sit beside him because he smelled. They gave him looks of derision and pity. A group of them laughed behind their hands when they heard his name during roll call.

"I thought you were a boy," Vincent whispered loud enough for me to hear as well as the kids around him, secure in his own masculine moniker. "How come you have a girl's name?"

They were feral in their manner toward him. Each one of them was deprived, insecure, and lost to some degree. But Kelly was flamboyantly poor, someone far worse off than they, someone they could torment easily. He was silent, shy, making himself an easy target, a scapegoat for their unhappiness.

The second week of school, when he came an hour early to sleep on my porch again, I brought him into the small, one-person staff washroom. The school was mostly deserted, especially at this end of the hallway. I felt furtive, the satchel heavy over my shoulder. I knew I should not be doing this. If I were caught, I could lose my job. A female alone in a bathroom with a little boy. It would look like something disgusting.

From inside my bag, I handed him the washcloth, towel, soap, comb, toothbrush and toothpaste. I showed him how to fill the sink with warm water, how to get the cloth wet but not dripping, how to brush his teeth. I gave him a little bottle of green liquid and showed him how he should put a finger pad of it onto his neck to make him smell good. I closed the door and waited.

When he emerged, he looked so different that I was startled. His eyes shone the same way his scrubbed skin did. With his hair combed off his forehead, the blue of his gaze was breathtaking. No one would glance down from that look to see his torn running shoes. The cologne obliterated the smell of his dirty clothing. He was a different little boy.

Wordlessly, smiling, he handed me the satchel.

"Maybe you should take this home," I suggested. "You could use this before you come to school."

He stared solemnly at the bag, then shook his head regretfully. "He'll just tear it up, Miss," he replied in a whispery apology. "But I can come early." The wistful smile chased away any misgivings I had.

His student record didn't tell me much. Both parents listed, a sibling too young for school, address in a particularly bleak area of the city.

I went to see Evelyn Phillips, his previous teacher. Most of the staff consisted of newbies, except for Eve, an enormous woman with a crown of silver hair.

She shifted when I asked about Kelly. The chair wheels squeaked in protest, matching the scowl on her face.

"That kid drove me nuts," Eve said. "So needy. He was always walking behind me. I nearly squished him several times." She chuckled alone. "His father is a monster. Beats his mother up all the time. She takes off to shelters a lot but he drags her back. Once in a while she gets him committed to 999, but then she always releases him." 999 Queen St. was the institution we all called the 'Insane Asylum'.

Eve yanked open the file drawer of her desk. She handed me a thin folder. "I wasn't allowed to put this in his record. I was supposed to throw it out. Here. Make sure you destroy it."

Back in my portable, I opened the folder. Inside were several newspaper columns. "Man Acquitted of Landlady's Murder" read one startling headline.

***

"Why'd they call you?" he asks, almost conversationally.

"It seems I'm your emergency contact for school," I answer, smiling. "The police called the school board – they called me. Are you okay?"

The police officers are getting restless. The one in charge leans over and whispers at me. "He's got about ten minutes. Then we're going to storm him, Miss. He's gonna get hurt."

Kelly ignores the exchange with the officer. "I'm okay," he says, shrugging.

"You gonna tell me what happened here, honey? I really need you to put down the gun. I'm afraid you might get hurt."

His head lowers and he stays so quiet that my heart pounds in fright. "Okay," he says.

"Okay what?"

"I'll put the rifle down. But first I want to show you something." He finally looks up and I see that his eyes are filled with tears. "Can you come in?"

"Sure," I answer, but as I step forward, the policeman grabs my arm.

"I can't let you go in there."

"Yes, you can. He's not going to hurt me. I'll go and find out everything. I can bring him back down, unarmed. You don't want anyone else to get hurt, right?"

It takes them a while and some heated discussion, but eventually I walk toward the open doorway. The steps are long and narrow. There is a terrible, putrid odour clinging to the walls. I know from experience that these stairs lead to two apartments, one where Kelly lives, the other where the landlady died.

***

My job became a combination of teaching lessons, keeping a little boy clean and fed, and trying to create a team out of a gang. As time went on, Kelly became more accepted. He didn't smell any more. He acquired a tiny bit more confidence. But he struggled with the schoolwork. He was morbidly quiet. The only person he walked with at recess was his teacher.

The newspaper columns that Eve gave me explained a great deal, but also left a waterfall of questions. Michael McKay was questioned about the murder of his landlady. "Someone in authority" told the reporter that Gertrude Rutledge was killed point-blank with a small handgun. "Neighbors heard the shot and discovered a three-year-old boy covered in blood, his father leaning over the body." A social worker claimed that Marjory McKay and Mrs. Rutledge had spent a lot of time drinking together. The motive, hinted the article, was jealousy. For a time, their son Kelly was sent to a foster home while both parents were investigated.

Eventually the case was dropped due to a lack of hard evidence. Kelly's mother, according to the same social worker, was attending Alcoholics' Anonymous classes and appeared to be rehabilitated.

Kelly was returned to his reunited parents. I couldn't imagine what this small boy had endured, what he had witnessed. At some point, his mother had given birth to their second child, a little girl.

Whenever I watched him in class, his little hands curled around a pencil, his lips pursed in concentration as he tried to form the letters, my love for him blocked any sense of objectivity.

One morning in November, Kelly didn't show up for school. I tried calling, but received no answer. After dismissal, I found myself trudging through slushy grey snow up Dufferin St. to the address in his file. At first I thought I'd made a mistake, but this was definitely the number: a fish and chip shop, its windows greasy with dirt, dead insects trapped between the panes. I opened the door and a bell tinkled. A tall thin man, dragons tattooed up his arms as though perched on tree limbs, sat reading a Playboy, his elbows on the counter. Head shaved, he wore an apron spattered with orange fat. When he looked up from the magazine, I knew where Kelly had gotten those ocean blue eyes.

These eyes, however, were thick with a sexual energy that created shivers of disgust and a frisson of fear that almost sent me back into the street. His gaze travelled from my eyes to my feet, a bullying scan that felt like an assault.

I managed to speak. "Hello. I'm Miss Stewart," I said.

Michael McKay looked back at me with a so-what glimmer.

"Kelly's teacher. I was wondering why he wasn't in school today."

The smirk deepened. "The kid misses one day and they make the teacher come and find him?"

I blushed, my secret exposed in that mocking glance. I gathered my self-righteousness and answered back, "Well, neither you nor your wife have had the chance to visit the school, so I thought I'd take this opportunity to meet both of you."

The statement elicited a chuckle. "Well, they're not here." McKay raised his eyes upward, indicating that their living quarters were above the shop. "She took the kids again. She does that when she's mad. She'll probably be back tonight, so you'll get the kid on Monday. Nice meeting you."

I stumbled back to the wind and slush, battered by the aura of disdain and misogyny that emanated from the man who'd fathered Kelly. It was easy to believe that he battered his wife, that he was capable of murdering his next-door neighbor in a fit of jealousy.

As Kelly would say later, that was one conclusion you could draw.

On impulse, I pulled open the outside door beside the restaurant, which I surmised must lead to the apartment. The stairway was steep, tile shriveled like dried orange peel.

The acrid scent of garbage and musty old carpeting, mixed with the grease from the kitchen below, assailed my nostrils. When I got to the top, a tiny landing presented two closed doors on opposite sides.

***

Kelly opens the door, the rifle flapping against the side of his leg as he walks, reminding me that he is armed and in an obvious state of agitation. For some reason, though, I am not afraid; I am sick with worry. The stench that punches into my face as we step into the apartment exacerbates the nausea.

There's a galley kitchen in front of us, laden with dishes and other detritus. A tiny dining room squats beyond that. To our left is a rectangular living room stuffed with an enormous couch and chair, a tattered carpet.

The main focus of my attention, the sight that drives bile into my mouth, is the bloodied, torn knot of bodies. One has a female shape, face down on the carpet, a crumpled heap praying at the feet of the other. The male is slumped in a chair, arms flung back, face a mass of red meat and white bone.

Kelly sits down in the chair opposite the gruesome tableau as though sitting in this chair, in this situation, is normal. He dangles the rifle as he would a tennis racket or baseball bat, objects of play that a boy his age should be holding. He is clearly exhausted yet frantic.

I stand beside him. When I put my hand on his shoulder, he flinches, then the tight muscles begin to give way to the warmth of my touch. "What happened, Kelly?"

He looks up at me and tears slide down his cheeks. I see shadows and layers of hurt flash through his eyes.

Curtains have been drawn over the bright hopefulness of the little boy I loved. The tears flow more freely. His shoulders begin to shake; his head drops forward. At the same time, he releases the rifle. It flops onto the carpet, useless, despised. I should call the police in now, but I don't. I sit on the edge of the chair. I enfold him in my arms, hold him as he sobs. I weep, too, for the loss of this child, afraid that he has altered his life forever.

"You don't think I did this, do you, Miss?" he says when he can speak.

I hesitate for a fraction of a second. "I don't know what to think, Kelly. I haven't seen you for so long." I make the last statement sound like a confession, a plea for forgiveness. I had stopped looking for him. I pause and there is a thick silence except for the drip of blood and tears. The air is a fog of metallic smells. "Why don't you tell me what happened?" He drops his head lower, he shakes it back and forth as though loosening the blockages, so I distract him, try to get his words started. "When did you come back here?"

"My mother owns this building. Mrs. Rutledge – the lady next door who got murdered? She gave it to her. Guilty conscience I guess. But nobody would buy it. We came back this summer to paint and clean it up, thinking maybe..."

At that moment, a bedroom door opens and footsteps approach. I stand up and stare.

***

Kelly did come back Monday. He, his mother and baby Jenna had spent one night away, he said, but they returned as usual.

"It was my birthday yesterday," he told me privately, "but nobody remembered. It's okay."

He said it casually, thin shoulders lifting nonchalantly, but I knew he was hurt. At lunch, I went out and got cupcakes. I persuaded Kelly to pretend his mother had sent them for everyone, to celebrate his special day. He grinned, blushing from his classmates' attention. The boys gave him a sportsman's slaps on the back; the girls giggled and said thanks.

I changed grades the next September and so remained as Kelly's teacher for two years. From time to time, he disappeared for a day or two. Slowly, he blossomed, still gangly and thin, but more open, talkative. Classmates befriended him, began to appreciate his sense of humour, his thoughtful, kind nature. They helped him with schoolwork, took turns coming early with Kelly to do the blackboards for me. Once or twice, I heard that he went to a birthday party at someone's house. No one seemed to question the fact that they were never invited over to his; most of them knew his circumstances were somehow too grim. Slowly he smiled, chuckled, played, grew. My colleagues called Kelly my "success story", but I knew that being the recipient of the light in his eyes made him a gift to me, not the other way around.

I forgot to be objective. I forgot that he was not mine to love and protect.

When the whole family left, including Dad, at the end of my second year, I spent many days that summer walking past the closed shop. It was a difficult time for Toronto; the economy sagged, the weather sizzled. In September, a request for Kelly's records arrived from a school in Saskatchewan. I knew then that I had lost him.

Grief taught me what my teacher training had not: maintain a distance from your students; be objective. Above all do not love them.

The transfer I had desired came a year later. I moved to a highly sought area of the city into an "easy" school, one with eager kids and supportive parents. I stopped walking past the shop on Dufferin. I married a man who already had two kids and didn't want any more. My children were all part time.

***

Jenna, who must be about ten now, walks into the living room. Her hair is a honey blond. Soft waves curl around her face in an unruly fashion. Her eyes are the same startlingly blue, fanned by long lashes and a creamy complexion. Her smock dress is faded and spotted with the bloody stains of death.

Jenna reaches for Kelly's hand, her eyes never leaving my face, her expression fearful and old woman sad. When she switches her gaze to meet his, the tears flow steadily. "Did you tell her what you did?" she asks.

He shakes no, no, no. My head spins as though I might faint. I fight to keep control, to stop myself from weeping. I want to scream. What happened here? What did you do?

Jenna looks back at me, her face flushed with grief. "I'll tell you, Miss. I'll tell you everything."

Kelly moans. I get down on my knees beside him, clutch his other hand. His sister squeezes into the chair next to him. We oddly mirror the tableaux of the dead, a trio of refuge in a gruesome scene.

"Tell me, honey," I coax her softly. "Please. Tell me."

"Mrs. Rutledge and my Dad, they were friends, you know?"

Jenna raises her eyebrows with knowledge beyond her years. I nod yes, I know what kind of friends they must have been. "My mother was really mad and jealous. So she shot her. Kelly saw it, but he was only little."

Kelly stops shaking; his hand clings to mine for safety. He sags; the secret spoken, the poisonous air releases from his chest. He looks more like a child without this burden.

"Everyone thought it was my Dad. Kelly never told the truth, even though he remembered a lot of it. He didn't want Mom to go to jail. Dad was mean. He always yelled and kicked us out of the house. Especially Kelly. Mom kept leaving him every time he talked to another lady. He would get so mad he had to go to the hospital sometimes." She takes in a shuddering breath. "In Saskatchewan, we hid in the basement most of the time when we weren't at school. Kelly took care of me."

"Just like you took care of me," Kelly says to me and my tears hover again.

"This dump wouldn't sell the way it is," the little girl continues, her mouth repeating adult words that had been flung against these walls. "Mom and Dad fought all the time. They threw things and hit each other." A sob sticks in her throat. She stops.

"It was really bad, Miss," Kelly says, looking up at me again, as though he has to convince me of the truth.

I feel the desperation, the overwhelming fear. Two young children perched on seats in a precarious boat as the adults stood and fought. Engaged in a boxing match of jealousy, never caring that they might pitch the whole family into dark water.

I see the bond of love between the siblings and wonder how that vine survived in such poisonous soil.

"Today Mom went crazy. She got her gun out. She made Dad sit over there and she made me stand beside him. When Kelly came in, he told her to stop, but she kept screaming and waving it at us." The sob breaks through. Kelly strokes her hair.

"I went into the closet and got my Dad's hunting rifle," Kelly continues for her. He points to it, at his feet, as though it frightens him.

"Kelly came and stood beside me," Jenna says. Her eyes are filled with pain but mingled within the blue are mists of pride and hope. "He told her if she tries to shoot us, he will shoot her. Then she…"

Kelly takes over again, when she can't describe the shock. "She shot him. Right in the face."

"Then she got ready to fire at me." Jenna's voice rises toward hysteria, as the horror sets in and the numbness wears off. I put my arms around her. She settles in against me, sobbing.

"So I shot her," Kelly says in a thick, miserable monotone. "All those times I thought my Dad was the crazy one, the one who drove her to do bad things. I protected her. All that time she was just getting worse. I didn't know she still had that gun. I don't know where she hid it." He spits disgust at himself, but his sister sees a hero.

"You saved me, Kelly," Jenna tells him, her small face full of wonder. "You saved me." She flings her arms around him and they cry together.

I give them a moment, then gently disentangle myself. "We have to go and see the police," I say as soothingly as I can. I hold out my hand. "But I promise you, nothing will ever hurt either of you again."

As I straighten, I see the future. I see my home with two full time children, from whom I will never be distanced or objective. Whom I will never forget to love.

They take my hand and follow me down the pitiful staircase into the sunlight. As we reach the open doorway, I hear the deafening tread of unison steps, the clack of triggers snapping into place. The reporters move forward with the crowd, flash bulbs in our faces. A wave of shouts crashes onto the shore of our triad, almost knocking us backward. I nearly drown in its strength, in the energy of capture and curiosity, in the fear that once again I will not be allowed to protect him.

I hold the rifle above my head and a hush rings out. I place it at my feet, where they can see that is now a harmless dead thing. I step forward with my cubs behind me, a she-wolf, fearless and defensive. I spread my arms to encircle the future that I envision. The pack facing us stops. Guns and cameras sink downward.

Then in a loud, clear voice, I tell the world what Kelly did.

An Alien Has Landed!!

By Tom Sullivan

"Welcome. Thank you for coming on such relatively short notice. Before we begin, I cannot express strongly enough that the information presented to you at this meeting, in this room must not, under any circumstances, be shared, even to the tiniest degree, with anyone not currently present. To make public any of the information we are about to discuss would be a serious breach of security and would be treated as no less than an act of treason. If you feel that you are not able or that you are not willing to comply, please indicate now and permission to leave will be granted." After a lengthy pause, the chairman continued.

"Let the record show that all present are in compliance with the stipulation. Thank you for your commitment. This meeting has been called to clarify recent rumours that a creature of alien origin has arrived in our midst from places as yet to be determined. This is something that the administration has strongly denied and understandably so. You have been invited here because collectively you represent our intellectual elite and, the administration feels, are therefore in a position to contribute to the evaluation of the situation at the highest level and offer input which may enable us to better deal with the situation.

Let me begin by saying that indeed a creature, undeniably of non-terrestrial origin has arrived among us. The reason that you have not been informed earlier is that we needed assurance that this alien was not one of an army of such beings or a forerunner sent to appraise our vulnerability and defenses. We are now satisfied that this creature is alone and poses no such threat. Of course it is early stages and we are continuing our examination as thoroughly and quickly as possible. For convenience we have named the alien "Exorbus", which you are asked to use since it does not carry all the baggage that the term "alien" implies. We felt that rather than go into lengthy details about Exorbus, it would be simpler to merely answer any questions presented by you. Of course much work is still being done and we will not be able to provide many details, but we believe that we can at least satisfy some of your curiosity. With that brief introduction, we will now entertain any questions." A number of attendees indicated the desire to make a submission. The chairman indicated one at random.

The questioner asked: "You said that Exorbus poses no threat of an invasion. Is there any possibility that this creature might carry some alien energy, which could pose a threat to us? Even something that our scientists are not equipped to detect?"

"We have present, a scientist whose field is just such an area and who will address this very valid concern."

The scientist adjusted into position to be able to answer, checked the odoriferity meter and began: "Of course all precautions are being taken. The subject is in total isolation and while certain gases and vapours have been extracted, there is nothing so far detected that could present a threat to our people. The procedure is to introduce primitive and then incrementally more complex life forms to gauge the effect that this creature has on them. We will not expose our population to Exorbus until we are totally satisfied that there is no threat to anyone."

Another questioner carefully adjusted his antennae and said: "I'm sure that all here present are just as curious as I am. Can you produce a likeness or at least provide a description. Does Exorbus have features similar to ours?" Attendees were relieved and amused that someone had expressed this. The answer was a bit of a surprise: "Actually, the physical attributes was one of that factors that allowed us to determine the origin of the subject rather quickly. Exorbus has a number of very distinct and, to us, unusual features." There was a long pause.

One attendee spoke up: "Well, don't keep us waiting. Provide details, please."

After a brief exchange between the chairman and fellow officials, the following information was provided:

"Well, most notably, the creature gathers information about its surroundings chiefly by means of electronic stimulus provided by light rays. It is able to absorb these into its body and determine a great variety of factors from this one sense alone. Another notable quality is the ability to gather and interpret atmospheric vibrations which provide information supportive of but distinctly different from the light rays."

"What about sense of smell?" asked an attendee.

"In comparison to the other two senses, this seems rather weak. While Exorbus itself gives off a number of distinct and sometimes unusual odours, his own ability to detect these is weak or even lacking." After dealing with a number of rather trivial and sometimes unanswerable questions, the chairman continued: "We have very little else to share with you at this time, but we are carrying out further examinations and will, hopefully, have much more to impart to you at a later date. Please be available to attend on short notice and please remember that none of this information is to be shared with anyone not currently present. Until next meeting, good-bye." The chairman then ordered that all odors in the meeting area be completely solidified and stored in secure containers so that they would be available for future reference. The containers were odorized as "top security" and carefully locked away.

After a sustained period of replenishing nutritional requirements the administrator met with two of the scientists who had been studying Exorbus. The administrator wasted no time getting to the matter at hand: "Well, what else have we found out about our new-found friend.

The scientist who specialized in restorative and maintenance studies spoke first:

"Well, when we introduced lesser life forms into the same compartment in which Exorbus is being held, in a relatively short time it absorbed the life form into its body."

"How could it achieve that?"

"Exorbus is equipped with an orifice near one end of its body and actually pushes the smaller life forms into that orifice, a bit at a time. It seems to utilize certain factors of the life form and thus the smaller life form sustains it."

"You mean that instead of a normal absorption of energy waves from solar sources, this creature actually consumes other living things?"

"That seems to be the case. We discovered this and have been providing the creature with various living material, but some it accepts and some it rejects rather violently. We are learning more about sustainable material as we go."

"What a surprise. Is the creature incapable of absorbing sustenance in the normal way?"

"It seems to benefit to a very limited extent from radiation but cannot maintain existence from this alone."

"Any other surprises?"

"Yes. We noticed that the creature at first lost some mass and we analyzed its body chemistry and found that it had a peculiar substance formed by the interaction of hydrogen and oxygen in its constitution and that this seemed essential to its survival. As you are well aware, hydrogen is quite plentiful, but oxygen is quite rare. We have been able to mine sufficient quantities to allow us to meet Exorbus's needs. When we first provided the concoction to it, it absorbed it very eagerly through its upper orifice and has consumed regular amounts of this mixture since."

"Can you tell us anything else about this peculiar substance concocted from hydrogen and oxygen?"

"Well, it is quite alien to us, but seems essential to Exorbus. It is made up of tiny molecules which conform to the shape of any container into which they are placed."

"That sounds ridiculous! You mean you can take a chunk of this stuff, put it in a box and it squirms around and takes the shape of the box?"

"Well, you can't really take a chunk of it. It has to be in a container and then you can move it from there to another container where it takes on the shape of that container."

"What is the container it is originally found in?"

"Good question. It seems to be extracted somehow from the atmosphere."

There was a great sharing of odors, which was a mixture of humor, disbelief and astonishment.

The chairman spoke: "I know these revelations sound incredible, but they are the facts as we have so far been able to determine them."

At the next meeting the chairman updated those assembled with the latest data and then asked for questions. The attendees were more prepared and the questions reflected this. The dialogue follows:

"Has the subject achieved replication?" Answer: "It is undoubtedly mature enough to have reached replication but there is no sign that it has done so. What's more intriguing, it shows no sign of being capable of doing so." This caused considerable exchanges around the room until one attendee asked: "But without replication, how could the population continue?"

The chairperson deferred to the expert in this field: "The subject seems to contain the requisite genetic material for replication but no mechanism to bring it to fruition. Very mysterious and we are still studying this."

When asked further about the sustenance procedure of Exorbus, one of the scientists present had another bit of updated information: "Exorbus periodically gives off residue in both solid and liquid form that seem to be by-products of the organism that he consumes."

"You mean instead of absorbing energy directly from the environment this creature has to consume lesser life forms and somehow uses these to rebuild itself and then discards the parts it doesn't need."

"That seems to be the case, yes." Antennae twitched around the room and conflicting odours made it impossible to distinguish any meaning.

"Have you been able to actually carry on communication with Exorbus?"

"We are making progress. Odours are pretty well lost on it so we have had to discover ways of transposing our odour emissions into atmospheric vibrations, which are comprehensible to it. This is going to take considerable resources and time and so we will suspend further meetings until we establish a reasonable level of communication with Exorbus. We will call another meeting when we feel we have sufficient level of communication and perhaps be able to find out something about Exorbus's origin and societal structure."

After a sustained period in which numerous scientists were employed to analyze Exorbus, another meeting was called.

"There is a great deal of material to cover concerning Exorbus and we ask that questions be kept brief and pointed. First we will call upon the scientist who has been in charge of maintaining the health and well-being of Exorbus. Doctor, would you make your presentation?

The doctor hovered and adjusted his antennae and began with a profusion of powerful odours. "We told you earlier that Exorbus sustains itself by the absorption of lesser life forms into its system and the secretion of unused portions of these. Also the product obtained by the interaction of hydrogen and oxygen has proved essential and we have been able to maximize a supply of both of these types of sustenance and Exorbus seems to be thriving rather well. In addition to this, our sustenance specialists seem to have inadvertently concocted a mixture of a variety of liquids and come up with a brew, which seems to raise the spirits of Exorbus considerably. This is being administered sparingly since, although Exorbus seems to enjoy this concoction, communication skills seem to be somewhat compromised by it."

"As to the matter of bifurcation, Exorbus seems reluctant to share information on this matter. Apparently instead of bifurcating in the normal way once maturity is established, Exorbites seems to have to have two members of the society contributing to the reproductive process. Just how this is achieved, we are not certain but Exorbus does have an appendage approximately mid-way in its body, which it somehow shares with another of its species and one of the two individuals then goes on to complete bifurcation. Just how they determine which one does this is unclear and Exorbus is not very informative in this matter."

The doctor paused and the room was filled with vapours indicating that there was considerable curiosity about Exorbus's society.

"You said that Exorbites have to sustain existence through the absorption of lesser life forms. Do we know how these lesser life forms are generated?"

"Apparently, there is a segment of the population dedicated to the production and preparation of these lower life forms. Strangely, although the society could not thrive without the efforts of this segment of the population, they are not held in very high regard. Actually many hardly share in the resources that they produce"

"What activity could they possibly hold in higher esteem than the very maintenance of their existence?" asked one individual.

"Well, it seems very strange to us, but in their society they have several levels of rewards. The highest level is for individuals whose image is projected throughout society and viewed by millions. Just what this achieves is by no means clear. The image does not seem to project any sustenance…. Just why these images are prized is a mystery, although they may provide some sort of inducement to bifurcation, but this is very unclear."

"Are there any other activities which are prized?"

"Yes, it seems that individual who show considerable dexterity with small spherical objects, referred to as balls, are very highly prized."

"Just what do they do with these 'balls'" someone asked.

"Well, they either keep them and refuse to let anyone else have access to them, or they hurl them from themselves using a stick or plate-like structure."

One of the members of the assembly rose and took the time to adjust his odoriferity meter to maximum production so his message would be received clearly and emphatically by all assembled: "This is unbelievable. I do not see any benefit in maintaining this creature any longer. I move that we either terminate its existence or at the very least, do our best to return it to its home planet as soon as possible."

The meeting place rather rapidly filled with various odors and it was concluded that the majority opinion was that Exorbus should, if at all possible, be dispatched back to its home. Much debate followed. There were those who felt that, since Exorbus found us once, his species would very likely be able to do so again and that they should therefore be terminated. It was thought that the best way to do this was to simply introduce a chemical process, which would cause the widespread disassociation of oxygen from hydrogen thus illuminating the compound, which seemed so essential to the survival of this species. This plan was voted down because, the majority felt, it could cause widespread suffering to a species which had really done them no harm. It was finally decided that terminating the species' ability to reproduce would eventually cause their kind to die out without any violent intervention. So, Exorbus was injected with a chemical composition which when released in his home environment would spread rapidly through the environment and render the species infertile. Exorbus would introduce this to his environment through the waste products that he expelled after absorbing other life forms. To speed things up, Exorbus was chemically programmed to expel larger than normal amounts of waste.

In the final meeting, the chairman reported as follows: "Exorbus has been dispatched to its home planet... at least we have done everything we can to achieve that end. It has received a life-sustaining infusion, which has rendered it into the same state that it must have been in on its journey here. We have adjusted its guidance program to exactly reverse its journey so it should arrive at least reasonably close to its origin. We have also included a mixture of the euphoria inducing compound so that when it wakes up it will be in positive spirits should all not go as planned. The only thing that we are a little concerned about is the radiation energy power source that we have installed to assure sufficient energy supply on the return journey. Our concern is that this needs a constant source of radiation of the type, which cannot always penetrate cloud coverage, which results from the condensation of the very hydrogen-oxygen substance, which seems essential to Exorbus's existence. If Exorbus's craft encounters one of these when trying to enter the home atmosphere, well, we doubt that it could experience a safe landing... but that's a risk that has to be taken.

On planet earth an announcement enveloped and shocked the world:

"We have an update on the condition of Vernon Beckford, the space traveller who dumped down unexpectedly in the Pacific Ocean. We are referring, of course, to the space scientist who was launched by the space agency in the latter part of the twenty-first century and had been presumed lost until his capsule splashed down in the Pacific Ocean some four months ago. Although Captain Beckford has undergone an intensive rehabilitation program, he is far from totally recovered. Still, he is considered somewhat of a miracle. After lengthy rehabilitation, his physical condition is superior to what the space medical personnel had expected. He is walking with assistance and his bone density treatment has responded surprisingly well. Surprisingly, he has shown a considerably greater tendency than expected to pass urine and feces. Other than that, Captain Beckford is in reasonably good physical condition. Mentally, however, the psychiatrists are baffled. The immediate surprise came as soon as he was retrieved from the capsule, but has just now been revealed. Captain Beckford was revived from his state of suspended animation in an intoxicated condition.... That's right! He showed signs of inebriation.

Although authorities believe that Captain Beckford's ramblings regarding beings which seemed to consist of little more than mist and odors are largely the result of the physical trauma encountered in space which has distorted his senses and memory, there is no easy explanation for the presence of alcohol in his system since careful research indicates that none was taken on board at departure and there is no known way to produce it in space. The investigation continues.

Dayanne Knight

By Catherine Astolfo

Dayanne was unable to adequately explain to the police why she took the letter. As a consequence, she had so far spent several sweaty hours in an interrogation room. It smelled like dirty socks and coffee breath, two things she was used to but couldn't abide. She was beginning to get antsy. Her explanation that she had been bored didn't satisfy them. The 'night in question' had been hot and sticky, so concentrating on unusual behaviour distracted her from sticky armpits and the stink of grease. They just couldn't, or wouldn't, understand the level of boredom that would drive her to notice such a thing.

The woman had been beautiful, slender, and sad. She sat in the Marilyn Munroe booth. Wasn't that enough to warrant attention?

Dayanne began to get tired of restating the same thing over and over. She decided to play games with the interrogators. It would be a huge episode in her journal.

The night 'in question', most of Dayanne's regular clients had been unfaithful, probably absconding to air-conditioned premises. There was no one to talk to, none of the usual miscreants to focus on. The letter had simply caught her eye. How could a police officer, whose job was never the same twice, empathize with the tedium of taking orders, delivering orders, cleaning up after orders? Thus they persisted in believing there must be a better, more nefarious, sort of reason.

Dayanne was a substantial kind of woman, with a couple of chins and a very large butt. Learning to skirt around the narrow aisles of the small restaurant without knocking plates onto the floor had been somewhat difficult, but she was a pro. She'd worked at the Sixties Café for nine years. Dayanne had not grown any smaller during that time and the café had not expanded, but she had a round, pretty face with soft brown eyes that gave her a youthful, innocent look. Fat was good wrinkle filler, she often said.

The design mimicked the diners of bygone eras, red leatherette benches, silver and black tables, the aforementioned narrow aisles, and old records glued to the walls. Posters of Elvis and Marilyn Monroe mixed with John F. Kennedy. The only Canadian pictures adorning the premises were of hockey players in full uniform with sticks.

Ten years ago, Dayanne's hopes of a different future vanished when her husband Greg fell down dead in their tiny galley kitchen. He'd left her with a load of university loans, never coming close to realizing both their dreams: that he would be a doctor and that she would be married to one. She was still paying off the debt, including the costs of his burial, still working at the Café—and still making tea in the same tiny galley kitchen.

Dayanne socialized with her customers to reduce the mind-numbing stupidity of her job. In secret, she loathed most of the people on whom she waited. This was a down market kind of place, yet because they were the clients, many of them felt superior. Sometimes she was tempted to spit in the soup or dig a dirty finger in the potatoes, just like they did on those reality shows. But she never did. Instead, she took note of their behaviours, clothes, habits, and pleasures, and she recorded them in her journal at home.

It was this same feeling of complete boredom that had her enormous rear glued to the chair in the institutionally green interview room. She neither asked to see a lawyer nor did she demand to be charged or set free. Instead, she began to enjoy the challenge. The police, who morphed into other officers as good turned into bad cop, were mesmerized. They couldn't bring themselves to believe her, but they couldn't turn away. Just like a deliciously juicy accident scene.

Dayanne repeatedly insisted that she took the letter because she was bored silly. Literally. She sometimes did silly things. Or told silly tales. Or sang silly love songs. One of the interrogators actually cracked a smile at that line. He was called Wayne Something. She decided he was the one to whom she could tell the whole story.

Her boredom led her to keep a watch on all her customers, she told him. She noticed things that her co-workers did not. She recorded everything about her clients and their antics in a journal. Dayanne secretly imagined turning these character sketches into a screenplay some day. Maybe the rights to the movie would take her out of this life she'd been dealt.

As though the insult of Greg's early death hadn't been enough, Dayanne had recently been forced to take in her mother. Which meant sleeping on a pull out in the living room, changing diapers, and bringing meals home from the restaurant. It also meant doing jigsaw puzzles every night, because that's what Anne loved to do.

This was the mother who'd had her first and only child in her forties. From what Dayanne could see, she'd done it in order to have someone to do her bidding. A kind of in-born slave.

This was the mother who'd named her little girl Dayanne. She'd obviously thought it was clever and different: a combination of her husband, Daman, and herself. Of course she couldn't predict that her daughter would go off and marry a man called Gregory Knight.

This was the mother who'd never worked a day in her life, whose house was mortgaged to the max, and whose husband had left her without pension or insurance. Like mother, like daughter.

She considered returning to her maiden name after Greg had passed, Dayanne said, but so far she hadn't bothered with all the forms and fees. So she weathered the jokes.

"Sorry to go on," she apologized, "but you see where this is leading."

Wayne Something appeared to have drifted off. He shook his head in bewilderment.

Dayanne was not offended, but she did wonder about the quality of training these days.

"Back to the letter, of course."

When he lifted one eyebrow, she had to connect it for him.

"Jigsaw puzzles? The letter? How the woman suddenly cut it to pieces and left it on the table?"

Finally, he twigged.

"Oh, I see. Like a jigsaw puzzle. Putting it altogether, you mean. Afterward."

She felt like giving him a high-five. He really was slow. Maybe not enough of a competitor after all. Though it still beat being at home doing another jigsaw.

"Exactly. I took it home to Mother Anne and we worked on it all evening. It's not easy putting words together like that. Not as if you have a picture to follow."

"So you are telling me that you took the letter as a new puzzle for your mother?"

"No, I'm telling you I took the letter because I was bored. Bored. As in bored stiff, bored to tears, bored to death, uninterested, fed up. I did everything because I was bored."

How many times did she have to say it? Dayanne was beginning to get a little impatient.

"Did you have to do something else to make it more exciting?"

Now it was her turn to misunderstand. "To make what more exciting?"

"Your life. Your journal. You aren't telling us everything you did that night. Did you plan to follow her?"

She laughed. "Don't be ridiculous. I'm not that bored."

"Bored stiff? Bored to tears? Bored to death?"

Maybe Wayne Something was a little less slow than she'd thought.

"Isn't it dinner time?" she asked. "My mother's going to be waiting. We have dinner when I get home from the day shift. Carl at the Café always has something left over for me to take. I really ought to be going."

"Come on now, Dayanne. You can't leave us hanging like this. You have to finish the story."

"Well...if you can feed my mother..."

"I'll see to it. I'll send some female PC's over. They'll be good to your mother."

"Can you and I get a pizza or something?"

"I don't see why not."

When he stood up, he was much taller than she'd remembered. She concluded it was those long, muscular legs. His hair was sandy, cut in military style, and his eyes were very blue. Quite a handsome fellow, perhaps just a little younger than she herself. And he did want her to stay. Dinner with a good-looking guy, she could write in her journal, and it would be true. The surroundings left a little to be desired, but she could leave that part out.

While they munched on the pizza, they talked about aged parents. His father was a widower, he told her, but Dad was enjoying life in a retirement village in Florida. Unlike Dayanne's mother, who was suffering from dementia.

"Dancing with women all night long, apparently," the officer said. "Once I went down there to visit and I could hardly keep up."

Wayne Something was single then, Dayanne thought, when there was no mention of a wife. Very interesting. She had to let the story out bit by bit, keep him thinking he'd established a rapport and was about to break the case. Maybe by then he'd be smitten.

Or at least deserving of a full page in her journal.

When they were sipping on tea for dessert, Dayanne took her story a little further than she had previously.

"The woman was lovely," she said. "Very petite, one of those slender bodies that men like."

"I like a little more substance myself," Wayne Something said.

Dayanne smiled demurely, as expected. He was a sly one after all. She was pleased.

"She had red hair with that kind of curl I envy. The kind lots of women pay hundreds of dollars for when they get perms. Her dress was a gorgeous rust colour, with no sleeves, but she was nicely tanned and fit, so it looked amazing. She wore a funky necklace and dangly earrings, this flashy silver colour that means they weren't too expensive. She ate the house salad and had a chicken breast with veggies."

"Was she friendly?"

"Oh yes, very. As I told you, or someone else here, I love to talk to my customers. Most of them love it, too. Lots of times, people ask to be seated at my tables."

"I'm sure they do."

"Anyway, she was really nice. And beautiful. I chatted a bit about the weather at first. It's a good ice breaker, you see."

Wayne Something was nodding now, since he'd proven he was actively listening by responding to what she'd said several times. Now he figured the only encouragement she needed was the movement of his head. Ha.

"She agreed that it was hot as hell, even asked how I could stand working in the Sixties' in that heat. I told her that I often had to go back into the kitchen and stick my head under the faucet, and she laughed. She ordered a bottle of white wine, chardonnay. I knew for certain then that she'd never set foot in the Café before. Our wine is dreadful, especially the chardonnay. But it was cold, so she drank one glass and then another. In the meantime, I delivered her salad. I like to leave them alone while they eat, it's only polite, but there weren't many customers, so I watched her while I cleaned tables."

When she didn't continue after his nod, he felt more interaction was required. "You watched her write the letter, then?"

A reflective question. Very good.

"Exactly. She had this pad and the pen moved really fast, covering the whole page. As if she were writing a confession, which I'm sure you've witnessed lots of times."

"People often write their confessions very slowly," W. S. said, then realized he shouldn't disagree with the interviewee at this point. "But not always. Go on, Dayanne."

"Anyway, she wrote fast. I could see that she didn't even pause to put in punctuation or capitals or anything. Except for the I's, but I found that out later. She looked so unhappy. I think there might've been a tear or two, but she was quick to wipe them away. She was like an actress in a tragic play, sitting there alone and grieving over something, in a blazing hot dive drinking swill. I could write a screenplay about her, I thought. She'd take more pages than most."

"Pages in your journal, you mean?"

She gave him a look that said, what else would I mean, you idiot, and continued. Her lack of response would serve as a message that some interruptions were unwise and unwelcome.

"So I kept a close eye on her. I drifted over from time to time, asking her if the salad was okay. Was the chicken hot enough? Did they give her enough veggies? Things like that. She always answered. Her voice sounded tired and sad, but every time, she was polite. Like she cared about what I thought. I was wondering if we could be friends instead of her being a character in one of my movies…"

A glance and raise of the eyebrows. Wayne Something had to be more careful of his facial expressions. Suspects noticed these signs.

"…when she suddenly took out a pair of cuticle scissors and cut the letter into tiny bits. It sat under her napkin through the whole rigmarole of getting the bill and paying and her getting change and tipping me. We talked a bit, about how it might rain, and she gave me such a sad smile…"

"What did she do with the rest of the pad?"

"She put it in her briefcase."

"She had a briefcase?"

"Oh, yes, didn't I mention that? Maybe to the other cop. I mean, police officer. She had a brown leather over-the-shoulder kind of bag. The ones messengers used to wear. It looked old. Her purse was small and blue. They didn't really match her outfit at all. So she didn't look rich to me. But then, rich people don't usually sit in the Sixties Café."

"What happened after she left?"

"I cleaned her table and put all the pieces of the letter into my pocket."

"You didn't know it was a letter at the time, right? Unless you read over her shoulder."

"No. You're right, I had no idea it was a letter. I had no idea what she'd written at all. I wanted to know, however."

"Because you were bored silly."

She smiled, watching his blue eyes dance with a bit of mischief. Oh boy, she could like this one. Maybe he'd agree to a free lunch at the diner once this whole business was over.

"You got that right," she said. "Bored and intrigued. I wondered what she'd written and why and to whom. All the questions any writer might have."

"I thought you were a waitress."

Dayanne was truly insulted by that remark and she let him know it. Her dark eyes could flash like a witch's, or at least that's what Greg had always said.

"When you get that twitch in her lips and your eyes bug out at me like that, I know I'm in trouble," he'd laugh, only partly in jest.

"I am a waitress part time. I'm just waiting for my screenplays to be accepted. Then I'll be out of there."

Back to the nodding.

She continued, even though she disapproved of his technique.

"Anyway…" The word should be a clue by now as to when he was barking up the wrong interview tree. "I took the pieces home to Mother Anne. I knew she'd be thrilled at trying to break the code. Even though she's got the dementia, she's unbelievable at puzzles. You should see the complicated ones she's able to put together. Sometimes the pictures are so lovely I frame them for her."

A knock at the door interrupted them for a moment. Dayanne waited while Wayne Something stuck his head out the door. This was probably the inevitable shift change. If he were truly committed, he'd refuse to leave and sit back down. Which, of course, he did.

Dayanne had to reward him for staying. "It took hours to paste the pieces together."

Wayne Something passed the glue-smeared page, now enshrined in plastic, across the table so she could read it.

"Is this the letter in question?"

"Oh my, we're being formal now. Yes, Officer, that is the letter I took. Mother Anne glued it together, so it's a bit sloppy. But that is the letter in question."

"Do you mind reading it into the record?"

"I don't mind in the least."

Dayanne thought she did a good job of it, considering there was no punctuation. She never stumbled on the words, her tone was interesting, and she emphasized or paused where necessary to clarify the message.

"my true friend,

I wish I could apologize to you for what I have done but of course I cannot I can never you are dead are you happy now did you even regret that decision before I ask you how this can be real I feel like a murderer even though it was your choice your plan it is not my reporting you must see the error remember how long it took you to convince me to go through with it you have been nagging me every day since the fall relentless as if an actor I was your lump of clay you molded me into your own design no one knew me too I did resist I did protest I begged you change course think of some other way to handle the situation but you finally wore me down you laughed at me you thought that I must agree with you I tell you try to stop your ways you will be in trouble they would shoot you were dead in a pool of blood and of guts at my feet you made my life become worthless I can not get out I am in hiding and alone that story cannot get recognized I could end up like a career criminal I am ruined if I'm unable to take this much longer I must follow I know I must not have suffered enough you win and then an end has to come."

"That's what we came up with, finally."

"How on earth were you able to read like that with no punctuation?"

"Well, we worked with these words for hours. We were finally able to read the entire thing."

"It's a pretty weird letter, kind of obscure."

"Well, when you are emotionally distraught, sometimes you don't make sense."

"What do you think the letter meant?"

"I think it meant her lover had been killed and somehow she was responsible. He got into a situation and was shot and she didn't stop him. The killers might even be after her now. I realized we had a time bomb on our hands."

"How so?"

Now that was a stupid question, she thought. Did she have to lead him through everything?

"Because of the suggestion that she might kill herself or be killed, of course," she said. "I must follow...an end has to come...you see? Her fellow was dead and she would soon be, too. By her own hand or by someone else's."

W. S. nodded.

"How did I know she or they wouldn't do it that very night? How did I know that I couldn't prevent it? It seemed like such a waste of a beautiful person."

"How did you find her?"

"The pad was a letterhead. Her name, address and phone number are right at the bottom. Here."

Dayanne tapped the lines with her finger. He knew perfectly well that it was there, but she was enjoying playing along.

"Can you describe what happened when you got to her apartment?"

"It was a dark and stormy night..." she began and he gave her the courtesy of that appreciative smile. "But it really was. Raining like cats and dogs, as they say. Her apartment is one of those old buildings, a walk-up, dark stairways and strong odours. Babies crying behind closed doors. Raised voices. All those elements that suggest poverty and dead ends."

Nodding. Good boy.

"I knocked, but the door was ajar and no one answered. I pushed it open, called out, said things like, hello, I'm the waitress from the Sixties Café, I'd like to help you."

Wayne Something's very blue yes were directly on hers now.

"But there she was, sprawled out on her bed, still so beautiful. The bottle of chardonnay was empty."

"The chardonnay?"

"Yes. I did see her slip the rest of the bottle into her briefcase. I didn't tell on her. I figured she was using the last of her money on a bottle of wine for some reason. Later I realized it was probably to kill herself."

Wayne Something did something curious. He held up a little baggie full of pieces of paper.

"Remember I told you about my father in Florida, Dayanne?"

It was her turn to nod.

"Well, besides dancing, he's an expert in jigsaws, too. Just like Mother Anne. Whenever I'm there, we play. We even play an online game together. Why don't you and I do a jigsaw, Dayanne?"

He took the pieces out of the baggie, but instead of allowing her to help, he began to expertly put them in order. As if he had a picture.

When he read it aloud, he did a good job of it, considering there was no punctuation. He never stumbled on the words, his tone was interesting, and he emphasized or paused where necessary to clarify the message.

"Day you are finally dead to me are you happy now I wish you were dead in a pool of blood and guts at my feet I cannot apologize to you you have been nagging me since the fall you were relentless I could not regret my decision I have suffered enough you made me feel like a murderer even though it was your choice your plan I know I can never be your lump of clay molded into your own design I did resist I did protest I begged you but of course you thought that if you wore me down I must agree with you I have become a true friend but you follow me you try to convince me to go through with it how can you ask this even if the shoot is not real I knew I could end up in hiding and alone if it did get out like a criminal worthless my career ruined and then my life will change course they laughed at me before you remember how long it took to get recognized for what I have done too I was no one every actor can tell you that story I'm unable to think of some other way to handle the situation you cannot win I must not take this much longer I am reporting you you must see the error of your ways you would be in trouble it has to stop it must come to an end."

She laughed. "Ridiculous," she said.

"My version makes as much sense as yours does, Dayanne."

"Hardly, Wayne. You know nothing."

"Actually I know quite a lot. This is what we've learned about your mystery woman who supposedly killed herself, Dayanne. You may not think your co-workers pay attention to the customers, but they do. Maria Costas had been in the Sixties' Café many times since October. You made friends with her. You discovered that she was an actress who had done some porno films previously. You wanted her to shoot one more of these, a script you would write, to show to a producer. You told her she could remain anonymous, that you'd make sure her face never showed. It was all about the script, not a real shoot, you told her. She thought about it, but then she found out that she had the chance to try out for a good part in a regular movie. When she refused to do the porno, you kept pestering her. Relentless."

He tapped the word on the page.

"What a silly story! And I thought I was bored. Here you are, Wayne, turning a tragic suicide into a murder."

"You poisoned the chardonnay. Convinced her to take the rest of the bottle home. She didn't cut up the letter at all. She wrote it hurriedly just before she left, and handed it to you. When she got home, poor Maria trusted you one last time. She drank the rest of the bottle and died as a result."

Dayanne laughed again and shook her head.

"I was curious about your husband's heart attack, too, Dayanne, so I went back to the police reports. Apparently he had drunk a half bottle of wine that night. Just enough poison to cause the fatal heart attack?"

"He was going to be a doctor."

"It says in the report that you were in shock when you were told that his insurance had expired. He hadn't paid the premiums. In fact, the police had to come to the insurance office and cart you bodily from the premises."

"He was going to make a lot of money as a doctor."

"Yes, but not quickly enough for you, right? We might not be able to prove you killed him. It's too late for that. But I think we can get you for the death of Maria Costas. It's funny, but we found two bottles of wine at her residence. One beside her bed and one in the garbage chute. What do you want to bet the last one has traces of poison in it? Oh, and the officers who took Mother Anne her dinner also took a search warrant with them. I would bet they've turned up a number of interesting things."

Dayanne's lips twitched and her eyes flashed. Her voice deepened and came out as a snarl.

"Get me a lawyer, Wayne. I have nothing further to say to you."

"No problem," Wayne said. "Would Mother Anne have drunk some wine next, Dayanne?"

She hissed at him and he left the room.

The officer outside the door high-fived him.

"Sure changed her demeanor, eh, Wayne?"

"Like dayanne knight," he answered.

The Bridge

By Tom Sullivan

For an eleven-year-old, it was like being on top of the world.

Harold's enthusiasm for adventure was infectious. At first, I didn't think that it was a good idea to make the climb to the railway bridge. The school had a rule against using the bridge as a short cut to or from school and even my mother, in her sober moments, would have thought it unwise. But Harold made it sound as exciting as an African safari.

That was the way it was with Harold. Most of the time he showed good judgment, but even if the scheme were ill advised and impractical, he had a way of convincing you otherwise. Harold wanted to spend this warm summer day, or at least part of it, on the trestle bridge. I had never made the climb before but Harold had. Several times: or so he said. I knew that he was partially testing me to see if I had what it takes to make the climb and stand at the most dangerous spot in all Tupperton... at least the most dangerous for an eleven year old... the very spot where, some three years later Harold would meet his death. I really didn't want to make the climb, but I couldn't admit that I was "chicken" and afraid of "a little height."

The climb was hard work and couldn't be accomplished without getting dirty. The forty-five degree slope was enough of a challenge, but the final fifteen feet was covered with railway slag that made footing difficult. Several times I stopped and looked down but that route didn't seem any more attractive than the road up, so I just kept going. The day was hot and a little humid and a circling wasp monitored the whole journey apparently convinced that if I should make it safely to the top all waspdom would be in instant peril.

The summit had its own rewards, though. I was struck by just how high up we were. I was reminded of the first time I climbed the ladder to the high diving board at the public swimming pool in Rosalea Park. From the perspective of the concrete apron, the high board looks little more than a couple of steps up, but once you made the climb the drop down looks parachutable. Well, the trestle bridge was many times more daunting. Harold arrived at the bridge level just ahead of me. When I got there I used panting as a delay tactic while I adjusted to the height.

I was allowed a period of orientation. Harold flaunted his experience by pointing out the two most readily discernable features on the landscape: the post office clock and Dale's chimney. The clock was about on the same level as the bridge but it was a strange feeling of superiority to realize that it was "over there" instead of "up there" the way you would view it if you were standing at the four corners.

Dale's chimney was on the north end of town and, although it was much taller than the bridge, it looked just like a single finger of brick sticking straight in the air as though it were making some rude gesture. Since no member of the public was allowed up on either the clock or the chimney, this was as high an elevation reachable within the limits of Tupperton without taking flight.

In order to delay the prospect of actually venturing out on the bridge I asked Harold to point out McHugh Public School. From this distance it looked like a shoebox. I took considerable time locating my home and, of course never came any closer than saying "It's way over there behind that growth of trees."

It was some minutes before I started to appreciate my position. I was still sweating and breathing a little heavily and the breeze, unthwarted by buildings, was a refreshing reward for having endured the climb. It didn't just cool you down and give you a chance to catch your breath, it reinforced a feeling of freedom...a feeling that you could do something that your parents and teachers couldn't do, even if they had wanted to. I ran my fingers through my hair and was surprised that it was so damp. Then I realized that sweat was running down my face and my tee shirt was a little wet at the chest and armpits.

At first, I was afraid to move, as though I were standing on the only piece of solid ground available and a move in any direction was a step into empty space. The bridge was for trains and didn't make any allowance for pedestrians. There were small signs saying "No Trespassing" on both ends of the bridge. There were no fences or barricades between you and a forty-foot drop to the creek below.

The creek was actually the Etobicoke River but nobody in town ever called it that. It really flowed only in the late spring when the countryside shook off its layer of snow and swelled the river for a few weeks. If you fell off the bridge in the height of the summer, you'd be lucky to hit water, which nowhere reached a depth of more than a foot or so. The river was, however, widest under the bridge. There was a set of twenty-two steppingstones placed so that all but the older adults could easily cross without getting their feet wet.

Of my friends, only Mousey Miller and Harold Smoulders would stand right at the edge of the railway ties and look straight down at the creek below. Harold did this well aware that others were admiring his bravery. Mousey did it with no more thought than he would have given to standing at a corner waiting for a bus. Others, including me, reserved an allowance of some two feet of tie between the edge and us. This meant that we stayed inside the parallel rails of the tracks as though they offered some assurance in case you tripped. They didn't.

The trestle bridge was built in the late nineteenth century and has remained relatively unchanged to this day. The concrete pillars have been reinforced several times and the river that flowed under it has been diverted and replaced by paved road, but the bridge itself remains as immutable as the memories I associate with it.

After that initial excursion, Harold and I used to play out on the bridge two or three times a week weather permitting. It was an exciting place to play but kids don't go there anymore since the accident. The original bridge obliged the trains, which ran twice daily between Toronto and Tupperton and therefore need only a single track. Harold and I used to talk about what would happen if one train was late and met another train crossing the bridge. We knew that they wouldn't let the two trains run into each other, but we wondered just what they would do. Kids who lived in the south end of town used to save a quarter mile by walking across the bridge to get to school. The school had a rule against going this way because the bridge doesn't have any guardrails or even any place to walk except along the tracks. But kids did it anyway. Until the accident. Since then they've built a high fence all the way down the tracks for quite a distance on either end of the bridge and now climbing over the fence with the barbed wire on top is a lot more trouble than walking the long way round to get to school.

For weeks after the accident we got lectures at school about how we should never play on the tracks and about how we should obey all the safety rules and all that. Every time teachers talked about it, I knew that they were really talking to me. They never actually looked right at me while they were talking and they pretended that they were not really talking about the accident. It is like they didn't know that I was there when it happened. But they knew. They all knew and all the kids looked at me while a teacher would talk about it. I was there when Harold was killed. I had jumped to safety but Harold didn't make it. It was all in the town paper: my picture, Harold's, and what I said. And what the mayor said about the danger of kids playing on the bridge. Everybody in the whole town knows all that.

But what I know, and they don't know, is that it was my fault. I killed Harold just the same as if I took a gun to him. I told the policemen and the guys from the newspapers the whole story, except for the end. All about how Harold and I were coming back from Buddy Burrows' place and how we decided to cross the bridge and how we stopped on the bridge to throw stones in the river. We'd get a handful of stones at the riverbank and then walk out to the middle of the bridge and throw them over one at a time. Sometimes we'd throw them at something, like maybe a piece of log floating down the river. Sometimes we'd just drop the stones straight down and see how big a circle the ripples would make, and sometimes we'd just see how far we could throw. Seeing how far you can throw isn't such a good idea because you can lose your balance throwing real hard. One time Billy Coles threw so hard he lost his balance and nearly went right over the side of the tracks and into the river. His friend, Al Evans grabbed him just in time. At least that's what Al Evans says. Billy says that's horseshit, that Al just says that to look like a hero and that he would have caught himself before he went over whether Al had been there or not. Point is, though, Al may not have stopped Billy from going over, but at least he didn't push him or something stupid like that to make him go over. Not like me with Harold Smoulders.

But, I didn't tell the police or the newspaper guys any of that. I just told them that we decided to throw stones off the bridge and we were there quite a while, going back a couple of times to load up with more stones from the embankment and carrying them out to the middle to throw them in. You had to be in the middle of the bridge because that's where the water is deepest and the river is widest in case you want to throw for distance. Well, we were doing this a while when, just as Harold was getting back with an armload of stones we heard the train. There was a whistle in the distance that meant that the train was just crossing the first line east and that it would be at the bridge in a few minutes. You can easily walk the whole length of the bridge in less than three minutes, so the sound of the whistle didn't mean that we had to panic. So we threw a couple more stones, just to show each other that there was no big hurry and that we weren't worried and because, well, what else could you do with a pile of stones in the middle of a bridge.

When we started to walk to the closest side of the river, Harold said, "If we go that way, we got to cross the bridge again to go home. I'm going the other way. Come on, we still got lots of time."

Since we always did what Harold said, we turned around and headed back the other way, toward the train. By the time we were half way back, we realized that the train was a whole lot closer than we thought. So we broke into a run and started to laugh because we knew that we'd make it but we also knew that we had to run. It was that mix of excitement and fright that makes monster movies and Ferris-wheels so neat. But in theatres and fairs, you know you'll survive. We knew we could make the end of the tracks and jump into the ditch but it was going to be close.

Suddenly there was an ear-splitting blast of the whistle and I could feel my heart start to beat like crazy and my skin get goose bumps and we both broke into a dead run and got to the end of the bridge just before the train arrived. I told everybody all that and it's all true. But I didn't tell them the rest. I didn't tell them anything about the last split second.

Harold and I used to play fight a lot. We'd be walking down the street and one of us would poke the other in the arm or bump into the other guy just for fun. The other guy would push or bump back and sometimes we'd end up wrestling for ten minutes or more and then get up and continue walking and talking as though nothing had happened. Well, this time, I mean on the tracks, Harold was running just behind me and to one side. When we came to the end of the bridge I stopped, and turned, and bumped Harold just for fun. It meant we had made it, we had beaten the train. It was like shaking hands and congratulating each other for winning. I didn't mean to hurt him and he knew it.

Just as I bumped him I jumped backwards off the track into the ditch. I kept my eyes glued on Harold as I fell backward and I saw the train catch him. I saw his eyes looking right at me. His mouth pulled almost into a grin as the train batted him straight up. His whole body seemed to change shape and blood came from everywhere. The whole time I could see his eyes. They weren't mad at me or anything, they were just there, only bigger and more intense than they should be. They were right on me even as the train hit him.

For a long time afterward, I used to see Harold's eyes like that and I'd even work them into a dream. I'd dream about something and my cat would be in the dream but the cat had Harold's eyes and they'd stare right at me.

After the accident, the school told my mom to get some counseling to help me get over the shock of losing my best friend and being right there and watching him die. So, I talked to this counselor and I told her almost everything: about the eyes and all, but I never actually told her about the bump. She asked if I felt guilty about Harold's death and I said no, and that is true. Harold wouldn't blame me if he were here right now. No, we bumped each other because we were pals and we liked each other. Harold would call it a goodbye hug or something but he wouldn't say I killed him, even if I did.

I've relived that moment for decades. Every detail of Harold remains vivid and precise. I remember his faint sweet smell, which, for some reason, recalls the harvested hay fields that surrounded Tupperton. I remember the nubs on his grey wool socks. I still see the lock of hair, slightly damp with sweat, hanging just over his left eye. And the eyes, oh yes, I see the eyes.

Often, in my mind, I change the thoughts that I had or the details of what happened on that day. As the days went by it became harder for me to believe that I didn't realize that Harold would die if I bumped him. I must have known. So why did I do it? Did I really bump him to celebrate our common success? I played the scene over in my mind and as we bump, I shout: "There, you superior son of a bitch." Or sometimes: "That's for beating me in almost everything!" or "That's for not letting Patsy Tomlinson look at me!"

I know that I never said any of these things, but I often run the reels in my mind. Sometimes, I play a different scene. I'm on the tracks with Harold and everything is very quiet and the train comes rushing at us, but it doesn't make any noise. When the train gets close time seems to freeze. I walk over to Harold and I reach up and take his head off his shoulders with both hands, just as I might lift a bowl from a table. Then, I turn and toss the head right at the train which seems to be frozen yet speeding towards us. When I throw the head, it turns and looks at me and I see those same eyes and the head almost smiles and then swells and there is blood everywhere. Sometimes I picture that at the last instant before the train hits him, Harold reaches out to me but I pull my arms away, making it impossible for him to be saved. I know that none of these things happened, but the truth doesn't seem to matter. What matters is that I caused the death of someone I loved.

I never felt as uncomfortable in my life as I felt at Harold's funeral. It seemed to me that everyone was taking turns staring at me both at the funeral home and in the church.

"That's the boy who was with Harold when he died. Harold and he were so close. It must be hard on him to be at his friend's funeral."

"I'll bet Harold's looking down on you right now, saying: ha! Ha! I don't have to go to school anymore." That's the stupidest thing anybody said to me at the funeral.

"Someday you and Harold will meet again and you'll take right up where you left off." Second stupidest thing.

I overheard Harold's grandmother talking to the minister and saying how she wished she had been stricter concerning Harold's choice of friends. She never did like me.

Those who knew who I was pointed me out to those who didn't. My mother said that I should stay at the funeral home the whole time that visitors were allowed to view Harold. Almost everyone who came talked to me. I didn't really pay much attention to what was said. I smiled weakly and agreed with them or I said something about what a great pal he was.

There was a large mahogany coffin that seemed much too big to hold Harold. Beautiful flowers, some in the form of wreathes and some in bouquets almost filled the room. My mother had ordered flowers to be sent to the funeral home but I had no idea which of the profusion of flowers was ours. The coffin was closed. When I approached to pay my respects I rather expected Harold to open the lid a crack and smile at me, as though he were still alive and this was just another secret we shared. There was a small kneeler beside the coffin. I knelt down and made the sign of the cross. I didn't pray. I didn't really think about Harold. I kept my eyes closed and thought that everybody in the room was looking at that kid who was with Harold at the last moment of his life. I felt sure that many of them were thinking that the wrong one died.

My mother told me that I must go up to Harold's mother and grandmother and tell them how much I will miss him. I didn't want to do this but there didn't seem to be any way out. I stood up and looked around and was rather surprised to see that no one even noticed that I had approached the coffin. People were standing in little knots talking quietly. Someone let out a quiet laugh. I started in the direction of the Smoulders family.

This was one of the few times that I ever saw Harold's mother in a dress. She usually was in a housecoat when I visited and she invariably carried a handkerchief in one hand and looked as though she were going to sneeze or cry, I never could tell which. Here, her wide eyes were looking all about as though the inside of a funeral home was not at all what she had expected. Before I started toward them, I saw the grandmother nod in my direction and say something to a tall slim man who stood just beside her. She had both sorrow and anger in her face. As I approached the family, the man stepped toward me and blocked my view. Up close, I was surprised to see how much he resembled Harold, except he was bald with just a fringe of hair around his ears.

"I understand that you are the young man who was with Harold when he died," he said.

I admitted that I was.

"I am Harold's uncle. The family wants to thank you for coming. I don't think that it is a good idea that you speak to Harold's mother or grandmother at this time. They are just too distraught. I will convey your condolences to them." With that he put his hand on my shoulder and gently redirected me away from the grieving mother and grandmother. I felt quite relieved.

When they lowered the coffin into the ground, I burst into tears. I would have bet anything that I wouldn't have cried, but boy, was I wrong. I just couldn't believe that Harold was dead. But I was crying mostly because I knew that he wouldn't be dead if it hadn't been for one stupid act by me. And since no one else knew this, I had to deal with it alone, and I found that almost unbearable.

When I got home from the funeral, I told my mom what happened and she stared at me for a long time as though she were checking to make sure I wasn't lying. When my mom wasn't spaced out on pills, she was good at this. I had a hard time lying to her. If I told her a lie, she'd just stare at me until I started to feel uncomfortable and then, if I were lying, I either confessed or started adding things that made it plain that I had made up the story. That's the way she stared at me when I told her what Harold's uncle had said. But I wasn't lying. Why would I lie about a thing like that?

After a long pause, my mom said: "They didn't want you to talk to them. Oh, my God." That really seemed to bother her, but she didn't say anything else about it.

The Monday after the funeral, I went back to school and it really felt weird. Most days when I got to school, Harold would already be there. We'd talk about what we did on the weekend or about some homework that I had forgotten but Harold had done to perfection and, if there was time, I'd copy enough of Harold's work to at least be able to say that I tried. But on that Monday morning, I went into the school and looked around and although I could name a lot of the kids in the halls, I really didn't know any of them. And none of them talked to me. I don't mean that they didn't say anything. They'd walk by and say "hi" and keep going, but nobody really talked. At lunch, I sat with some kids from my class, but I was definitely on the edge of the group. There was a fat girl in our class who no one treated as a friend. She wasn't disliked, she was just not included. I now knew how she must have felt.

After school, I walked part way home with Borden Weekes. He carefully avoided the subject of Harold and chatted away about some science show on the radio. He asked if I listened to it even though he knew I didn't. When I answered, he went on to explain that some astronomers had discovered something new about the planet Pluto, as though I cared. Borden was trying to fill the time until we got to his place.

When we got there, Borden turned and looked at me and said, "He was my friend, too." And then went into his house. I rather resented him saying that.

No one talked about Harold or his death to me, but stories and rumors went around the school and the town. One rumor had it that Harold and I had a fight on the bridge and I hit him and he fell back and hit his head and that I ran and left him there. Another rumor said that I was never on the bridge: that I just watched from the side and saw my friend die. Some said that Harold was too smart to go onto the bridge unless I talked him into it. As though I could talk Harold into doing anything he didn't want to do.

Whatever the reason, kids avoided me. I don't mean that they walked across the street when they saw me coming, I just mean that they never kidded with me or told jokes or included me in any way other than as part of a group. Whether they thought I was a bad influence, dangerous, or just bad luck, parents didn't want their kids chumming around with me. I had never felt so alone in my life.

Branch 45

By Catherine Astolfo

It's Bingo Night. Frank doesn't feel like going, but he knows they need him. He gives out the Bingo cards. Somehow, when Doris was alive, it used to be fun. Now it seems like work. This must have something to do with getting old. He straightens his tie in the mirror.

A young boy's face gazes out at him. He looks dashing, his hat tilted to one side. The light khaki colour suits him well. He stands stiff and proud, uniform pressed, shoulders straight, as they snap pictures of him. He laughs loudly, slaps them on the back, shakes their hands wildly. No one can tell that he is frightened. His stomach knots again. He fights the tremor in his hands.

Tenderly he polishes the buttons of his jacket. He looks dapper for an old guy, he thinks in his favorite British accent. Right as rain, old bean, and all that rot. He checks the envelope for the Bingo cards. His parcel safely under his arm, he walks out the front door and marches toward the Legion.

They march smartly up the main street of town. People crowd the sidewalks, waving flags, clapping, shouting their support. They do not look from side to side, but they know the women's faces are stained with tears. Once in a while someone glances toward a loved one. But mostly they keep marching, the train station looming nearer. His stomach knots again.

Frank goes in the back door of the building and ends up in the kitchen. He can hear them gathering already in the main hall. "Where's Frank?" he thinks someone says. They are always waiting for the Bingo cards. He wonders who will do this when he is gone, who will care. He hopes he won't be one of the men they wheel up to the table to play every Tuesday night. Reaching under the counter, he grasps a small brown bottle. He tips it to his lips and drinks deeply. For a little courage.

"Jesus, look at the tits on that one!"
They are leaning out the window of the train. Frank turns to the young man beside him. Face red, eyes beaming, he waves furiously to no one in particular.
"Have a snort, kid," he says to Frank.
Frank nods. He likes this tall, outgoing man, and he does not wish to offend him. The dark liquid burns on his tongue.
"That'll get your blood flowin', kid. Mine's Harry, what's yours? Put 'er there, Frank, old pal. I think we'll be together for quite some time. Have another snort. It'll get your courage up."

Franks peers out into the meeting hall. Already most of the seats are taken. For a moment he relishes their panic that he is not there. Then someone sees him. It's Al Grant.

"Get over here, Frank! Where the blazes you been? We're nearly ready to go."

Frank slips the little bottle inside his jacket and goes out. There isn't any booze until the Bingo is over. Wouldn't want to offend the ladies and the old gents. Usually he and Al head upstairs afterwards. They have a good time with the darts and the shuffleboard and the cards. Just good clean fun.

They start playing cards shortly after the train moves out of the station. It's a bumpy, crowded train full of young men. Very quickly Harry has them organized. He sets up the games, figures out the rotations, and tells the jokes. He also puts limits on any betting. Doesn't want anyone to go broke in the first hour, he says. For some reason, he treats Frank like his kid brother. Has Frank sit beside him or follow him around. Frank doesn't mind, in fact he likes it. Makes him feel less lonely. The liquor in Harry's bottle seems endless. Frank's tongue already feels thick and his head is light on his neck. He tells Harry maybe he'd better lay off a little.

"Oh, hell, kid. It's just good clean fun. I mean, Jesus H. Christ, we might be dead by day after tomorrow. Why not live it up now?"

Franks starts moving down the tables, giving out the Bingo cards. He has an apron with pockets to collect the cash. "Twenty-five cents a card, ladies, gents." His voice sounds like it belongs to someone in a carnival. He always gets some giggles with it. "We aim to please at good old Branch 45."

The McClary sisters are here as usual. Flory is tall and thin, gangly like a giraffe, while Rose is stooped and fat. The only thing they have in common is their hooked nose. They smile at Frank as he passes by. He pats them on the back. How would you like me to stick my dick up your arse? he thinks.

He turns to old man Romsey, who is a veteran of the First World War. Frank thinks he must be more than a hundred years old. No one knows whether or not he enjoys Bingo, he's blind and deaf and hasn't spoken for years as far as Frank knows. His daughter Mildred sits stuffed in a chair beside him, placing his chips. She doesn't even lift her head as Frank goes by and gives her two cards.

And here's Mrs. Crowe, Mrs. Virgin Mary Frank calls her privately. She purses her small lips and gives him a queenly smile. She's head of the Ladies' Auxiliary and as such deserves a little respect, don't you know. "Evening, Madeline, hope your luck's good tonight." You probably never got lucky in your whole life. Your poor dead husband, rest his soul, probably had a wet noodle for a dick.

"Well, hello there, Leo, how ya doin' old pal?" Frank reaches out a hand to the thin man across the table; he smiles and tells Frank he's not doing too badly, can't complain. But Frank remembers when Leo was big and dashing, not withered in a wheelchair. Frank finds it hard to look at him.

As night comes, the car is hushed. Some of the boys sleep in seats, while others sit around and talk in quiet tones. Harry tells stories about the war. He's been over once before, sent home on a sick leave.

"It's hell," he tells them. "The enemy's everywhere. You gotta lie in the ditches forever. Then when your turn comes up, you leap out and pray to God you'll get them before they get you. And the stench of the dead bodies...we was marchin' up one road in Italy and the corpses were strung out everywhere. After a while you sorta get used to it, you know...we kept pokin' at them with our bayonets..."

His eyes glaze over a little. Someone asks Harry if the war is going to last much longer.

"Christ, no. We got 'em by the balls. I'm surprised we're even goin' over there. I think we'll end up bein' a mop-up team."

There is a groan of regret. Everyone is supposed to want to be where the action is. Frank's spirits lift. He hopes it's over before they get there. He has a horror of coming home maimed, or of not coming home at all. He tips back Harry's bottle. Relaxes a little more.

"Under the B, Number 2." Al looks real formal up there. Face expressionless and serious. Frank leans against a wall and waits for someone to yell Bingo. Then he has to go up and check the card. Once in a while he sneaks a nip from the bottle. He takes a good look around the room. He knows most of the people here. Many of them are women, mainly because it's Bingo night, but also because there are a lot of widows. It's shocking to think of all the men he knew, now dead. Maybe even forgotten. He thinks it's a strange twist of irony that Doris died first. She was so young. It's over thirty years now. He feels a twinge of remorse. Funny to think that when he's gone, he'll only have these people to remember him. Not even a son or daughter to shed tears. Only this collection of oddments. He takes another longer drink from his bottle.

As they board the ship, Harry pokes Frank in the ribs. "Have one more, kid," he says and winks. "Just think. They could blow us outta the waters before we even get there. Imagine that this collection of asses might be the only ones attending your funeral."

Frank grimaces and swallows. Harry thinks he is being funny. Frank's stomach is knotted even tighter.

They cram onto the dank grey craft and are assigned to bunks or floor space. Frank finds himself in a room with Harry and three other guys. It is a room originally designed for two. Harry immediately organizes the sleeping arrangements, especially rotation of the beds. Frank notices that Harry makes sure they sleep together on the floor and together on the bunks. He is pleased. If they sink, Frank figures, at least he'll die with a good friend like Harry.

"Bingo!" Frank leaps up and heads toward the claimant. It's Major Brown of the Save-the-Souls Army. She's dressed in her uniform, filthy brown hair tied on top of her head, glasses resting on her flat bulbous nose, face studious. Al calls out the numbers and Frank checks them. She's out by one.

"You're full of shit, Frank," she hisses, her deep man's voice a whisper in his ear. "You're a bloody cheater. I'm going to flatten your head when we get outta here.."

Frank looks down at the huge hands spread on the table in front of her. He calls up to Al that it all checks out. Frank and the Major gaze at each other for a moment. Her dull brown eyes blink out at him from behind the thick glass like caged birds. Frank calls out in carnival style that the lady wins fifty bucks. He empties his bottle.

Harry pulls another bottle out from under his mattress. Frank, his tongue loosened, asks Harry where they come from.

"Hell, kid, I got connections all over this tub. Don't worry about it. We'll never run out."

Frank starts to protest that he's not worried about...

"Yah, I know. Deal the cards," Harry says.

They have been out at sea for twelve days. There have been no problems, no attacks, no high winds, nothing. Just water. Once in a while they spot land, but at such a distance they cannot tell where they are. Rumours fly. Some say they are taking a long route to avoid the German ships. Others claim they are lost. Still others say the war is over and they can't decide whether or not to land.

Harry says that the last theory is probably correct. "They're likely sorting through a big mess there, Frank. We'll have to wait and see if we're needed."

While Al continues to call, Frank solves three or four problems quietly. There are always arguments as to whose card is on the right, especially when four to eight cards are involved; heated discussions because someone spoke when the last number was read out. The Allen Street Gang (they are all neighbours) always buy six to eight cards each. Nearly every Bingo they come to blows over which card is whose. Frank calmly straightens it out, then tells them what numbers they missed.

Old Mrs. Malone puts a bony hand on his. "You're wonderful, Frank," she whispers. "We'd never do without you." When she wins the hundred dollars, she slips him a ten.

Frank sighs. They need him so much around here. It's a good thing he didn't decide to stay home after all.

Harry and Frank are propped up against the bunk. Frank listens as Harry tells the same story night after night.

"Then she asks me, see, would I like to do something different? And I say, well, sure, what do you have in mind? Then she teaches me these positions, I

mean she must've been a gymnast or something, you should've seen the moves..."

Frank's eyes are stinging. He feels the lift of the boat the way he has never felt it before. Even if he had something to add to Harry's story, he can't say it. His mind drifts and his head floats. He thinks he has been this way for days.

"Twelve days and twelve nights," Harry whispers. "That's how long we've been here, old buddy, old pal. And all that time without pussy."

Fingers are fumbling at Frank's belt, then his zipper. His head lolls stupidly to one side. He cannot raise it, he is powerless. He falls over sideways and lies there, feeling the rock of the ship. His stomach turns. Someone pulls his trousers down. Franks tries to struggle, tries to move. Pain. Tingling. Pleasure. He is still. A harsh ripping sensation. Then pleasure. He feels Harry gyrate, hears him moan. Frank jerks with pleasure. Hot sticky liquid seeps down his legs. He closes his eyes. Fades away. Shame in his mouth like bile.

Al takes a few gulps from his glass, then positions himself in front of the board. He squints. No one speaks. Frank taps his fingers silently. Al lets the dart fly. A roar goes up from the small group. Double one! Al leaps over a chair and throws his arms around Frank, flushed with the victory.

"Get your sweaty paws off me, Al."

There is silence for a moment. Everyone remains still. Except the eyes. They all gaze questioningly. Then Al laughs.

"Christ you get ornery when you're drunk, pal. Let me buy you a drink." And he walks to the bar.

Harry begs Frank to believe him, he didn't mean it. He was drunk, carried away... Harry throws his arms around Frank, flushed with pleading.

"Get your sweaty paws off me, Harry."

Harry releases Frank's shoulders. Frank walks away, leans over the railing of the ship, stares at the water. Fourteen days. Just sea, endless blues and browns and greens. Night and day. Stars and sun. And the rock, rock, rock, of the boat.

Frank doesn't speak to Harry for two days. Then he begins to miss something. Not just the friendship, the jokes, the cards, the diversion from sea and sky. But the liquor. Frank suddenly realizes he can't take another day without a drink. He goes up to Harry and asks if he can join the card group.

Harry's face lights up. "Let me buy you a drink, kid."

He makes a space for him and hands him the bottle. Frank takes a long drink. That night he sleeps better. The only thing that bothers him is the dream. In it he feels the pleasure, the tingling sensation. Hot liquid runs down his legs.

Kyle Thomas wipes a few tables and collects bottles. He tells Frank and Al that it's time to lock up.

"Screw off, Kyle," Franks says pleasantly.

Al hoists Frank up by the arm.. Frank nods stupidly as they stumble through the door.

"Hey, listen Al, tomorrow's the big meetin'. And they're havin' a Bingo first."

He laughs loudly in the still starless night. Then he frowns.

"Have I got the cards, Al?"

Al feels Franks' jacket pocket, assures him he has them.

"Good, good. They need us, you know."

Frank lives just up the street from the Legion. Al tells Frank he better make sure he gets home okay. Frank stumbles up his front step, feeling his way along the side of the house in the dark. His stomach knots. Wrenches. He leans against the brick and vomits into the garden. His nose and eyes and throat sting. He feels the sob rise.

He kneels on the grass, then falls over, sideways. Fingers fumble at Frank's belt, then his zipper. His head lolls stupidly. His stomach knots. Someone pulls his trousers down. Fingers. Pain. Tearing. Burning. Hot. Liquid. Pleasure. Frank lies there for a long time, crying soundlessly.

Twenty-one days. The captain assembles them on deck. Tells them they are, at last, going to land. The war is over. They will be a clean-up crew, he says, assigned to different areas of Italy and France. He reads out the names of those being sent to Italy. Frank is one of them. Harry's name is read out for France. The boys have a big party that night. They aren't happy, they say, that they won't see any action. But at least they'll be off the boat. The troops for Italy go first, tomorrow. Stories fly. Cards. Jokes. Booze, lots of it. As if they haven't been at sea for three weeks. They laugh loudly. Shake hands. Slap each other's backs. By dawn, it is quiet. Most of them lie slumped all over the lower decks.

Harry and Frank are propped up against the bunk. Frank listens as Harry tells the same story.

"Then she asks me, see, would I like to do something different? And I say, well, sure, what do you have in mind? Then she teaches me these positions, I mean she must've been a gymnast or something, you should've seen the moves..."

Frank's mind drifts and floats. He thinks he has been this way forever.

"Twenty-one days and twenty-one nights," Harry whispers. "That's how long we been here, old buddy, old pal. And all that time without pussy."

Fingers fumble at Frank's belt, then his zipper. His head lolls stupidly. He falls over sideways and lies there, feeling the rock of the ship. His stomach knots. Someone pulls his trousers down. Fingers. Pain. Tearing. Burning. Hot. Liquid. Pleasure. Frank lies there for a long time, crying soundlessly.

Timothy Edward Everly

By Tom Sullivan

Timothy Edward Everly, or Teddy as he was un-affectionately known, was "conceived out of wedlock." That was the quiet church and school hush between adults and sufficient explanation for his unseemly behavior. It was understood that the deliverer of the news was sharing this secret for the first time and only to the receiver who, obviously, would let the information go no further. Somehow, every adult in Tupperton was sufficiently informed to be able to act appropriately...whatever that meant.

Teddy's mom, Madge Connor, was a waitress at Percy's White Corner Restaurant, which was neither white nor on a corner and not much of a restaurant, for that matter. Madge flirted and joked with every male that came into Percy's and had a reputation of being what the good citizens of Tupperton called "loose."

Teddy's dad was a shoe salesman at Bradley's Shoes. Bernard Everly was a diffident little man obviously seduced by Madge and credited with fathering her child. Bernard, who was the antithesis of a lady's man, was at first a little proud of the fact that he had fathered a child and accepted paternity as fact. Bernard Everly was thirty-four and still single at the time that the elements that would make up Teddy came together. He did what was expected of him and married Madge.

Married status didn't really mean much to Madge, except for her job. In the depression era, a boss could fire a waitress for becoming a single mom. Madge needed the job, so she needed a husband. Bernard was the most available, if not the most desirable candidate.

Bernard had worked at Bradley's Shoes since he graduated from high school. He lived with his parents until they both died within a year of each other and the family home transferred to him. There were also some modest investments sufficient to support Bernard for life had he chosen to live very frugally. He didn't.

Bernard dressed well. Proper dress shirt and bow tie that, he was proud to say, was the genuine tie up one, not one of those phony clip-ons. He felt that it was his duty to wear fashionable, but not ostentatious shoes. Bernard was short in stature and a little on the chubby side. Rather soft-tubby, which was minimized with the right attire.

His other somewhat extravagant luxury was the odd fifty-cent cigar smoked on a park bench on a Sunday afternoon or at the lacrosse games on a Saturday night in the summer. Bernard was fond of lacrosse even though he had never voluntarily played any sport in his entire life.

He was a valuable employee of William T. Bradley who had inherited the shoe store from his father. William T was a rather poor salesman and hated waiting on women who seemed incapable of reaching a decision without strong prompting. William T was not a strong prompter. Bernard was…and he was both informative and sufficiently obsequious to make him the lady's choice when buying shoes. He accurately anticipated the latest trends. William T had the good sense to put Bernard in charge of ordering shoes from the wholesalers. Bradley Shoes gained the reputation as the store from which the wealthy and fashion-conscious ladies of Tupperton would buy their shoes.

Bernard fussed over his customers and always insisted that they try on several pairs of shoes before choosing. He dispensed suggestions and compliments with equal sincerity. It was rare indeed when a woman would walk out the door not having spent considerably more than was intended. William T could not survive without his top employee.

To Bernard, it was a job. He didn't particularly like shoes and he wasn't very fond of women. His boss had sufficient business sense to recognize Bernard's value and paid him a good salary. Bernard could have earned even more money in one of the big shoe stores in Toronto, but he didn't like driving and would not have tolerated the daily commute. It never occurred to him to leave Tupperton.

Timothy Edward Everly, known almost from birth as "Teddy," was born prematurely, but still weighed in at over six pounds. Rather than unite the couple, the arrival of Teddy seemed to drive them even further apart. Madge still pictured herself as a party-girl not yet ready for the role of mother. Neither Bernard nor anyone who knew him thought of him as the fatherly type.

Teddy wasn't a year old before Madge resumed her flirtatious ways. Before the boy was two, local gossips claimed inside knowledge of Madge's continuing illicit affairs. She had little use for Bernard once they were married. She often humiliated him in public, calling him porky and dropping humorous remarks that hinted at his lack of virility.

Bernard at first tried to cope. He would laugh at Madge's remarks when with friends; laugh and hurt. He was strangely afraid of Madge. He felt trapped. He soon grew to hate his new life. But divorce was not easy to obtain in those years. As far as Bernard was concerned, impossible for him to afford even if it were. Besides, Bernard felt that most adult males in Tupperton regarded him as a bit effeminate since he was such an expert on ladies' shoes. He thought that his marriage to a real looker like Madge gave him a more masculine image and he was not going to ruin that. He would keep up the appearance of the happily married man even though many people suspected a sham.

Besides, Madge was only part of the equation. If he divorced, what would be his legal and social responsibilities with respect to their son? Madge would demand support for both herself and Teddy. Even if he had little communication with his wife, he would have to support this child for years to come. Resentment grew and spawned suspicion. He became convinced that the child could not be his. The boy didn't look at all like him. Strabismal eyes and reddish cheeks which Bernard saw in neither his family nor in his wife's. The real father was probably laughing at him for having assumed this burden. The unidentified father was beyond retaliation, but Bernard had plenty of opportunity to exact vengeance from the bastard offspring, the real cause of his imprisonment.

Madge was often late coming home from work. She would claim that her boss wanted her to work overtime. Or, she would explain that a friend came into the restaurant and they sat and had coffee when her shift was over and talked for hours. Sometimes, she'd get a phone call from an old girlfriend over in Georgetown and she'd drive over there in their ten year old Ford and not arrive home until the early hours of the morning. Pretty fancily dressed for meeting an old girlfriend, Bernard thought. Whatever the cause of her absence, Bernard was left with the baby.

Bernard visualized Madge meeting with one of sundry boyfriends and having drinks in some hotel room. She would be telling her lover how she trapped her poor stupid husband into thinking that he had gotten her pregnant and had practically begged her to marry him. This wasn't true, of course, but it might well be how she would relate the story. Perhaps she was meeting with Teddy's real father and they were roaring with laughter over how that poor witless sap was supporting his child. Well, maybe that bitch was treating him like a doormat, but her bastard son would be made to pay the price.

With the mother gone, Bernard refused the boy's every request. No, he couldn't play. No, he couldn't look at a book. No, he couldn't have paper and crayons to color. Bernard assured the boy that his mother was gone from the house most of the time because she hated her son who couldn't do anything right. If the child cried, Bernard would mock-cry along with him and call him "sucky-baby."

As the child reached about eighteen months he started to show rebellious behaviour. He would push his food off his high chair tray onto the floor. He would kick out at anyone trying to clothe him. Bernard knew better than to hit the boy, causing bruising. Instead, he would grab the boy's short hair in his thumb and forefinger and pull sharply until the boy's behaviour was acceptable.

About a year before Teddy was born, and while Bernard was still living alone in his inherited home, he had bought some rat poison to get rid of a few pests that had invaded his garage. The unused portion of the poison sat, tightly sealed, in his garage until one day three years later, when he opened the tin and, unsure of the contents, wiped some of the substance on a rag that happened to be close at hand. The label on the tin had become obscured and Bernard, without his reading glasses, wasn't quite sure what he was dealing with. He sniffed the rag and found the odor noxious. Just as he pulled the rag away from his nose, he heard the phone ring in the house and quickly stuffed the rag into an empty bell jar, shoved the lid tightly on the container and returned the container to a cupboard. He then ran to answer the telephone.

It was William T. wanting to know if they had ordered the new ladies casuals in dark brown. They had already received delivery and the shoes were in the stock room. Bernard had to explain to William T how to find them and had to stay on the line until he was sure the shoes were found. Bernard forgot about the container and the rag until one night, when Teddy was almost three years old, Bernard went into the garage. Before he turned on the light, he detected something glowing lightly in a corner.

The first thing that occurred to him was that some fireflies got into the garage, but it really wasn't the season for them. He turned on the light and deduced that the glowing had come from a bell jar that stood on a shelf. He retrieved the bell jar and examined it. It had a cloth stuffed inside. He took the jar over to the overhead light in order to have a better look. He stared at the jar for several seconds and noticed that the cloth inside had several smears of some substance on it. Did those spots glow in the dark? He turned off the light and, sure enough, little spots of glowing light emanated from the cloth in the jar.

He thought for a few minutes and then remembered the incident of discovering the substance in the container and that he had put the cloth in the jar. Apparently, the substance had a phosphorescent quality. The cloth had glowing spots that actually seemed to move if the jar was just slightly rotated. Bernard searched the garage shelves and cupboards until he found the container and determined that its contents were rat poison. He smeared the cloth liberally with the substance. Then he turned out the lights again. The effect was dramatic. The glows from the rat poison waved eerily in the dark. He stared at it quite enjoying the effect. In the dark, the waving form looked almost alive. Like a ghost.

Teddy was barely four years old when he decided that he hated his parents. His mom paid little attention to him. His dad had let the ghost stay in the house and hide under the bed. And both of them complained about almost everything he did. His mom had a whiny irritating voice that worsened when she smelled of cough syrup. But while he hated his parents, he somehow was not afraid of them. All his fear was of the ghost.

His mom didn't know about the ghost and if she ever found out, the ghost would do some really terrible things. He asked his pal Peter if he believed in ghosts. He did. But, not in the one under Teddy's bed. Peter insisted that ghosts didn't live under beds. They came down through the roof or they walked through closed doors. And they talked to you about what would happen if you weren't careful. Teddy's ghost didn't do any of those things, but he knew his ghost was real and it stayed under his bed. He had seen it.

His dad kept it locked in a big jar and showed it to him and told Teddy that if he didn't behave, he would have to let the ghost out and it would do dreadful things to him. And the ghost could too! Teddy would lie on his bed knowing that the ghost was waiting in the jar beneath him. He thought every bump and rustle of wind that he heard was really the ghost trying to get out of the jar or at least reminding Teddy that he was in there.

One night, just after Teddy got into bed, he noticed that everything was quiet for the longest time. Teddy hoped that maybe the ghost had gone. Should he peek under the bed to see if it was still there? Better not. Another ten minutes of silence. Maybe just a peek. He slid out of bed and got on his hands and knees. He lifted the edge of the bed cover just as his father came into the bedroom.

"So, you want to bother the ghost do you?" Bernard snapped out the light and the phosphorescent material glowed. Teddy recoiled.

"I'll show you what happens to disobedient little boys who bother the ghost." He slid the bell jar from under the bed.

Teddy leaped up on the bed and drew himself up in a ball tight against the bed board. He wrapped his arms around his shins and kept his eyes glued on the glowing, waving figure in the jar. In the dark, he couldn't see his father slip the lid off and wipe his finger on the cloth inside.

Bernard made sure that the finger had picked up a small trace of the phosphorescent substance. He pushed the finger to within an inch of Teddy's nose.

"The ghost doesn't like cheeky little boys," Bernard hissed.

Teddy's head was shaking so much that his lips accidentally came in contact with the extended finger. Teddy felt an acidy taste and rubbed his mouth with his sleeve and then pulled the covers over his head and sobbed.

"I won't bother the ghost again. Honest I won't!"

Bernard didn't say a word. He put the lid back on tightly and slid the bell jar under the bed and left the room.

For two days, Teddy was quite sick to his stomach. His mother told him that it must have been something he ate at school and gave him a lecture on not sharing food with other kids.

"I can't afford to take a day off work every time you pick up some little bug."

She left the house without even checking his temperature. Bernard assured the boy that it was the ghost's way of showing him his displeasure.

It was a long time before Teddy would challenge the ghost again. Sometimes he would almost forget about it, but when his father wanted immediate obedience, he needed only remind Teddy of the consequences of non-compliance. Teddy would physically shake as he obeyed.

It was Madge who broke the ghost's spell. She usually left the household chores to Bernard. He was a bit of a neat freak, but she was willing to live in a mess. In a rare fit of house-cleaning fervor, Madge decided to give the house a thorough vacuuming. When she vacuumed under Teddy's bed, she found the jar.

Teddy had just started junior kindergarten and was shocked to find the jar sitting on the kitchen table when he came home one day. But the ghost was gone. In the bright light of day, he could see that there was an old rag inside the jar but no ghost. He approached the jar slowly intently focused when his mother entered the kitchen.

"What the hell was that doing under your bed?" she demanded.

Teddy mumbled incoherently and kept staring at the jar. His mother lifted the lid as casually as she might lift the lid from a pot on the stove. She had been cleaning in the bathroom and wore rubber gloves. She reached into the jar and pulled out the old rag.

"What the hell are you saving this piece of garbage for?"

Again Teddy gave no answer.

"I swear to god, I sometimes wonder if you are all there!" his mother said, carrying the rag to the back porch and dropping it into the garbage container. She then returned to the counter, took the jar to the sink and proceeded to wash it.

Teddy just gaped. What had happened to the ghost? He went up to his room and, after some hesitation, decided to look under his bed. Maybe there had been two jars. He got down on his knees, checked to make sure that his dad was nowhere in sight, and peaked under the bed. No jar.

Teddy woke up in the middle of the night. Maybe the ghost was still under the bed without the jar. Maybe he had missed it when he looked earlier today. Maybe you couldn't see the ghost in the daytime. Teddy pondered this for a long time before he slid out of bed, checked in the hall to make sure no one else was about, and then dropped to his knees and peeked under the bed. No jar. No ghost. Teddy got back in bed and didn't know whether to feel relieved or further threatened. Once out of the jar, the ghost might be anywhere. Teddy got out of bed again and went downstairs, stopping frequently to assure that he was alone and that the ghost did not lay waiting for him around the corner or at the bottom of the stairs.

He entered the kitchen. All seemed to be perfectly normal and very quiet. The night-light gave off an unfriendly glow, but nothing like the ghost. Teddy crossed the kitchen floor practically on tiptoes in order to disturb neither the ghost nor his parents. He stood for a full minute in the doorway that separated the kitchen from the porch. He reached up and paused before he turned on the porch light.

He kept his fingers on the light switch as though he anticipated some disaster that he could instantly control with the switch. His eyes swept the room and his gaze settled on the garbage can. That's where she had thrown the cloth. Was the cloth where the ghost lived? How could that be? With the fingers of his left hand still on the light switch, he reached out with his other hand and grasped the lid of the garbage can. He held it firmly for several seconds as though listening for some reaction within the can. After a minute's hesitation, he lifted the lid with one quick pull.

There was the rag that his mother had thrown out. Teddy stared at it for some moments waiting for it to react in some way. But it was just a dirty rag. Was that what the ghost wore? No, ghosts only wore white sheets. This rag had never been white. And it was stained with some sort of grease. A ghost would never wear that. Teddy's parents' bedroom window was directly above the porch. Teddy heard a faint cough and immediately turned out the porch light in order not to attract his parents' attention. He still had the garbage container lid in his hand. He looked in the container.

There was the ghost. Teddy gasped and almost cried out. But sanity prevailed. Why was the ghost in the garbage? Teddy decided he would risk disturbing his parents and turned the light on again. No ghost. Just garbage and the rag. Teddy lifted the rag by the smallest bit of the corner that he could get a grip on and switched the light on and off several times. Each time the rag would glow just like the ghost.

Teddy dropped the rag back into the garbage container. He turned out the light again and stared for several minutes at the contents of the container. He turned the light on and off several more times. He finally replaced the lid, turned out the light and made his way across the kitchen and up the stairs to his room.

Just as he turned to close his bedroom door, he saw his father come out of his parents' bedroom and start down the hall toward the bathroom. Teddy had never noticed before what a small man his father was. Teddy went to bed and thought some more about his discovery. "The ghost isn't IN the garbage. The ghost IS garbage." That night, he resolved that he would not let his dad, or anyone else, rule him or hurt him again.

"Mrs. Everly, I must have a serious talk with you concerning Teddy. This is the third time that there has been an incident reported of his anti-social behavior. Would you please come to the school on Thursday afternoon? Fine, I look forward to meeting you."

"Mrs. Everly, I am afraid that there has been little or no improvement in Teddy's behavior. I'm sorry that circumstances forced you to miss our last appointment, but I think it is important that we meet. What time would you be able to come? Fine, I'll see you Tuesday right after class."

"Mrs. Everly, I am beginning to get complaints from other parents with respect to Teddy's aggressive behavior. We have made two appointments, which you, unfortunately, were not able to keep. I must insist that you come in to see me at your earliest convenience. No, Mrs. Everly, the week after next will not do. If you cannot make it in before this Friday, I will have to exclude Teddy from class until we have had a chance to talk."

"Mrs. Everly, thank you for coming. I was hoping that Mr. Everly might also be able to attend."

"Mr. Everly has no interest in Teddy's schooling. He and Teddy never get along."

"I'm sorry to hear that. Mrs. Everly, I'm afraid that Teddy has shown some strong anti-social tendencies. At times, he is downright aggressive. The other day, he poked a girl in the face with a ruler. He said she had laughed at him."

"I don't know what to do with him. He and his father don't even speak and now he is driving me crazy."

"Have you considered private counseling?"

"I can't afford private counseling. If I could, I'd get it for myself. He doesn't need it. He has everything he could possibly want."

Surprisingly, Teddy pretty well did have everything he wanted. He could handle his father. He had a source of money. And he was convinced that nobody, but nobody, could hurt him ever again.

Teddy constantly found ways to irritate his father. Bernard came home one day to find the garage floor sprinkled liberally with motor oil and an empty oil container in the garbage.

"Teddy, how did that motor oil get on the garage floor?"

"Dunno." But Teddy had the trace of a smile on his face similar to what a young lad might have if a girl asked if it were he who had sent her flowers.

"You little bastard!" Bernard struck Teddy across the face, but not hard enough to remove the trace of the smile.

Another time, some pages were torn out of a book that Bernard had been reading. Once, glue had been poured on the handle of his screwdriver and needle nose pliers. Teddy denied any involvement.

Bernard shouted at Madge, "I can't do anything with him. Beating him doesn't work. He won't even cry. He just keeps that goddamn smirk on his face."

Sexual encounters between Bernard and Madge were rare. Madge would arrive home late after having a few drinks. Bernard would be aroused from sleep. Mating, rather than lovemaking, followed. Through some miracle of sexual chemistry, Madge gave birth to Amelia. The baby girl weighed almost eight pounds and looked just like Bernard.

This certainly did not make the child pretty, but Bernard doted on her. He felt that whatever fates there be had rewarded his patience by sending his own daughter to him just when the future seemed nothing but bleak. He did not, however, feel any greater affection for his son or wife.

The night shift at the restaurant was even more desirable to Madge after she returned to work following Amelia's arrival. All shifts paid the same, but the evening shift was busier and more customers meant more tips. Since the start of the war, more people had jobs and tips improved accordingly. The evening shift also meant that Madge had to spend less time at home with Bernard and Teddy and more time alone either with Amelia or with any friend who might drop by for a daytime visit. Unlike Teddy, Amelia had brought out the motherly instinct in Madge. She enjoyed playing with her and even changing and feeding her; chores she always abhorred and avoided as much as possible with Teddy.

Amelia was the one source of happiness that Bernard and Madge had in common. Unfortunately, it wouldn't last. Amelia was three months short of her first birthday when disaster struck. Madge was at home. She was due at work at four that afternoon. Bernard was at the shoe store when he received a frantic call from his wife. Madge was screaming hysterically and Bernard couldn't understand what she was saying, except that Amelia's name periodically came through the sobbing gasps. Bernard dropped the telephone and raced home to find Madge kneeling on the floor beside Amelia's crib. Almost immediately behind Bernard was Dr. Barry.

"Mr. and Mrs. Everly, it is a phenomenon known as crib death. It happens at a greater frequency than most people think. The baby just stops breathing. We don't know why it happens, but we are quite sure that there isn't anything you could have done to prevent it. You should not blame yourselves."

But Bernard did blame himself. One month after Amelia's simple funeral, William T. Bradley called at 9:30 a.m. and woke Madge out of a sound sleep.

"Madge, I certainly understand that Bernard is undergoing a difficult time right now and we are quite willing to make allowances for absences, but I would sure appreciate it if Bernard would let us know ahead of time when he is going to be off for the day."

Madge groggily apologized and hung up the phone. She called out to Bernard but got no answer. She decided that he would just have to handle Mr. Bradley himself. She went back to the bedroom and slumped back down in the bed and slept.

At five o'clock that morning, with Madge sleeping deeply beside him, Bernard had awakened and made a life-altering decision. He took a single suitcase and quietly packed a carefully selected wardrobe, called a cab and was taken to the bus terminal. He boarded a bus fill with commuters making the daily trek to their employment in Toronto. He arrived in Toronto just at 8:30 and had no trouble arranging for a room at a hotel near the terminal. He ate a light breakfast at a local diner.

At about 10:30, he contacted the manager of one of the larger shoe stores whom he had met the previous summer at a sales convention. After brief pleasantries, Bernard asked the manager, Arnold Knowles, if he could call around to see him. They arranged to meet for lunch at a restaurant convenient to Arnold's store. Bernard returned to his hotel room, showered, put on his best suit and went to an adjacent barber for a trim. He arrived at the restaurant looking quite the businessman.

After chatting about latest trends and general market conditions, Bernard explained that he had decided to move to Toronto and asked Arnold if he needed any sales help at his store. The manager knew of Bernard's expertise and hired him on the spot. Bernard returned to his hotel room and wrote a short notice of resignation and posted it immediately to William T. Bradley. Bernard continued to live in the hotel until he found a comfortable second floor flat in an old Edwardian-style house within two blocks of the store. Bernard never set foot in Tupperton again, nor did he ever again see Teddy or Madge.

Madge woke late on the day that William T had phoned and prepared to go to her four to midnight shift at the restaurant. Bernard had seemed consumed with guilt over the death of Amelia. Madge refused to accept any responsibility whatsoever. Only she knew that she had had a visitor the day Amelia died and that Amelia was alone for well over an hour before Madge checked on her and found her not breathing. The doctor said that there was nothing that could have been done and Madge accepted that.

Bernard, who wasn't even in the house at the time of the child's death, would break into spontaneous sobs and mumble self-deprecating assertions of guilt. Madge was never fond of Bernard's company but since the death, being at home when he was home was something she sought to avoid if at all possible. Another advantage of the evening shift.

Teddy seemed almost unaffected by Amelia's death. He found his father's behavior pitiful. He had long regarded his father as a weak, spineless creature, almost not worthy of any attention at all. Amelia died. Everything dies. Why make such a fuss over someone who could not even speak or do anything? Teddy decided he didn't need to cause any more problems around the house. Both parents were reduced to a level beneath his consideration. Besides, he was getting real recognition from the kids at school. He knew they didn't like him, but they now treated him with a certain respect that sometimes bordered on awe.

The genesis of this newfound admiration was an incident that occurred a couple of months before Amelia's death. In those years a perfectly acceptable form of punishment in schools was the strap. Each teacher was issued a strap to be kept in the teacher's desk. Some teachers used it liberally, others not at all. Students soon got used to the routine. In some classes you could get away with almost anything. In other classes behavior had a higher priority than learning. In this respect the strap produced the desired result in students. Except Teddy. He seemed to actually choose the toughest disciplinarians' classes to demonstrate the most outrageous behavior.

Every pupil in that class remembers the day the teacher strapped Teddy. Some have since told the story dozens of times. Here's Jenny Bennett's version.

"Most of the time, when you talked about Teddy, you were careful who you talked to because most of the things you'd say about Teddy would be about how you hated him and what a rotten thing he did to you or your best friend. You didn't want to say this to anybody who might tell Teddy. This day was different.

"Teddy was a little older than I was but had been held back at least one year. He was sitting behind Mary Lou Henry in art class. Mary Lou was a sort of fat girl with long black hair that hung down her back in pigtails. Well, Teddy took his art scissors and quietly snipped away a few hairs at a time until he cut right through Mary Lou's left pigtail without her even realizing that he'd done it. Then he dunked the pigtail in the glue pot so that it stuck up like one of those feather pens you would see in a movie about Ben Franklin or somebody. When Mary Lou saw the pigtail, she let out a scream and grabbed the sides of her head to be sure that the pigtail was really hers. Screaming was something that Mary Lou never did. She was always shy and blushed even when the teacher asked her a question. The teacher thought that Mary Lou must have been stabbed or something and rushed down the aisle to Mary Lou's seat.

"Once she got there, she never even asked what happened. There was the single-pigtailed Mary Lou, the glue pot with a pigtail sticking out like a small flagpole and Teddy sitting behind with almost a full smile on his face. The art teacher who everybody knew was one of the toughest teachers in the school went redder than anybody had ever seen her. She hauled Teddy to the front of the class and right in front of everybody she had him hold his hands out while she yanked the strap out of her desk and gave Teddy eight good whacks of the strap on each hand.

"Most of the kids in the school had at least seen the strap. And you knew when someone was going to get it. The teacher would call out a student's name and say something like: 'Harvey, step into the office for a minute.' The teacher then would reach in the drawer and do what could be done to hide the strap while it was removed from the drawer. Harvey would get up and follow the teacher. The 'office' was a small room between each pair of classrooms and each teacher in the two rooms had a desk that faced each other and were rammed together. Kids almost never went in there except to get a lecture or get the strap. Even when teachers just talked in the office, the students could hear most of what was said, unless they whispered.

"When a student got a lecture from an angry teacher, you could hear everything that was said. When a student got the strap, you could hear every stroke. When this happened we kids would become dead silent and count the number of whacks. Sometimes, Harold Smoulders would stand at the front of the class and pretend to be counting the whacks swinging his arms the way you'd see a boxing referee count when a boxer is down. We would all listen to hear any screams or sobs. If you got the strap, you wanted to go back to class without crying or you'd be called a sissy.

"It was alright to come out of the office shaking your hands or rubbing them on your pants, or even blowing on them, but don't have a tear in your eye. Sometimes a kid would still be crying at recess and his reputation as a sissy was sealed forever. Tom Stollery had the worst reputation because he only got the strap once but he had started to cry on his way into the office and sobbed so loud afterwards that the teacher sent him to the washroom to 'wash up' so she could go on with teaching the class. Although everybody had seen some kid right before and right after getting the strap, nobody ever actually saw someone get the strap. Until Teddy.

"Then the kids were really surprised at what they saw. For one thing, Miss Straunich, the art teacher, looked quite funny swinging her right arm a way back behind her head and bringing the strap around in a great circle. Roy Crawford said she looked like a baseball pitcher trying to deliver his hardest possible pitch, except he was doing it in a blue flowered dress and with a hair bun instead of a baseball cap.

"But the real surprise was Teddy. He kept his hands straight out in front of him and as flat as could be. He never pulled his hand back even slightly when the strap hit his hand. He kept them out there after Miss Straunich finished until she told him to put them down and then he only did it very slowly, like he was saying: 'Are you sure you don't want to do anymore?' But what really wowed the kids and bothered Miss Straunich was that Teddy kept smiling the whole time. It must have hurt but he seemed like he was watching some kind of trick that you might see a clown do at the fall fair. Not only that, but just as the teacher was telling Teddy to put his hands down, a school bus pulled into the school yard just outside the classroom window.

"Teddy asked as politely and sweetly as any teacher could expect: 'Miss Straunich, do you think the school is going to get new buses next year?'" Miss Straunich snapped: 'You have a lot more to concern yourself with than school buses, young man. Now return to your seat.' Teddy returned to his seat and never even so much as shook his hands or blew on them. From then on, he was still feared but now he was also something of a hero."

Thank you, Jenny.

Teddy figured out a very clever way to get money. He did as little as possible around the house, but the one chore that he was always willing to perform was shopping. Madge would send him regularly to the local grocery with a list of items and with as close to the right amount of money as she could find in her purse. Teddy, as soon as he arrived at his destination, would take the list and do a sweep of the store, finding first the smallest items on the list and carefully concealing them in a pocket or under his shirt. He then selected the rest of the items and went to the cashier and paid only for these. He would often ask the cashier to give him the change in just quarters or dimes and nickels.

When he got home he would put all the goods, including the hidden loot, on the kitchen counter and leave the change (minus the cost of the purloined items) there too. He was much more anxious to do the shopping in the winter when the increase in his revenue was directly proportional to the increase in the number of pockets.

Teddy didn't like physical education. In the good weather, phys ed was held outside in the school yard. Students changed into gym shorts and shirts in the change room in the basement of the school and then reported outside to the gym teacher. Two classes were always assigned phys ed at the same time so that the boys and girls would have separate classes, deemed essential at that time. The girls were on the south side of the school and the boys were on the north side where the baseball diamonds were marked out.

Since there were two classes, it was difficult for gym teachers to take attendance. Often the teacher just looked up and down the collection of students standing in rows. The teacher would pretend to check with names on a clipboard. To take attendance properly would have taken far too much time. In other words, it was fairly easy for a student to skip Phys. Ed. It was even easier for Teddy because the teacher was usually quite pleased to see that Teddy hadn't showed up and ignored the absence.

This suited Teddy just fine. Usually he would just stay in the change room or sneak out behind the boiler room and engage in his new-found pleasure, smoking. One day, when Teddy had been enjoying his strap-defying reputation for a couple of months, he slipped out behind the boiler room only to find that he was out of cigarettes. He could wait. He would buy some on the way home. He would have no trouble doing this because, in those days, there were no restrictions on selling cigarettes to kids, provided the kid claimed he was just on an errand to buy them for some adult.

But Teddy realized that he had another problem. He hadn't brought any money with him that day. He decided that rather than just waste his time waiting for the Phys. Ed. class to end, he would sneak home and get the money from his stash under the books in his bedroom and then be able to buy the cigarettes on his way home. It wouldn't be safe to buy them before the end of school because the store clerk might ask why he was fetching cigarettes in the middle of the afternoon. He might phone the school and report the student to the principal.

Sneaking off school property in the middle of the school day required a bit of strategy and some risk. You had to stay close to the boiler room wall and then make a dash across an open stretch of some fifty yards before reaching the weeping willow trees that provided a perfect screen for any student walking down Elliott Street during school hours. It was the fifty yards of open space that presented the problem. Teddy had an idea. Instead of staying by the wall, he walked casually out to the field directly toward the girls Phys. Ed. class. He kept his eyes on the ground and his head going back and forth as though he were looking for something on the ground. Once he passed the class of girls, he made a quick right turn toward the trees as though he had found what he was looking for. Teddy was soon on the street and on his way home.

Teddy entered the house and expected to hear his mom's soft snore as he passed her bedroom. She was working the night shift and probably hadn't got up yet. Her door was closed. Instead of her breathing, he could hear voices. One was a man's voice and the other was his mother's. At first, Teddy thought that his father must have come home in the middle of the day.

But why would he do that? And why would they be in the bedroom together softly talking and laughing? They wouldn't. It wasn't his father. His mother was in there with another man. Teddy felt rage and then a forced calm. He would not let himself care. He crept by the door, went to his room and found the cash he needed for the cigarettes. He also picked up an old pack from a jacket pocket and found that there were two cigarettes in it. He left his room and glanced in where the baby was sleeping.

Almost as an afterthought and with very little hesitation, Teddy entered the room and stood for a moment watching Amelia lying on her stomach. Both his parents loved her. She had received more love in her nine months than Teddy had received in thirteen years. No ghost. No neglect. Teddy reached into the crib, put his hand on the back of the baby's head and shoved her face down into the pillow. The baby tried a stifled cry and waved her arms for just a minute and then was still.

Teddy left the room as calmly as if he had just gone in to make sure she was sleeping comfortably. He got back to school with just ten minutes until next class.

Frank, Jacob and Me at Midnight Mass

By Tom Sullivan

There weren't very many Catholics in Tupperton when my parents moved here in the late 1930's and there aren't a lot more now fifteen years later. There was Father Coughlin, of course. He always used to warn us kids against unnatural sex acts... whatever they were. Father Coughlin smoked and I always wondered what was so natural about smoking. The other one hundred percent Catholic was old Mrs. O'Hara who taught us catechism on Sundays after Mass and who seemed to think that the worst sin a kid could commit was not going down on one knee every time you walked in front of the altar. Of all the kids I knew, only Gerry Paceo was Catholic and he served as altar boy at all three Masses on Sunday.

There were other well-known Catholics in town but I doubt if Father Coughlin had them in mind as models. If one of my friends knew that I had been to church, he would ask me if I had seen Frank Donahue or Jacob Von Goerton there. Then he'd laugh.

Both Jacob and Frank were known as Catholics within the community although this stretched the definition to the limit. To the local puritan Protestant element they were proof that God considered Catholics as the Lord's lost sheep, whose souls had been bent by the "jiggery-pokery" of papist teaching. They were to be both pitied and avoided.

The only time that Frank Donahue overtly declared his faith was during the Orange parade, held in Tupperton each July twelfth. This parade was one of the two large parades held each year in our town. The other was the Santa Claus parade, which Frank ignored. But on July twelfth, he would stand on the main corners in downtown Tupperton and shout obscenities and admonitions at the participants in the passing parade about their bigotry and how the battle of the Boyne was a lie, the Catholics really having been the victorious party. He went ignored, but not unnoticed. It was the only time that Frank ever showed any measure of aggression.

Frank spent a lot of time on the main street in Tupperton and people were known to cross the street to avoid encountering him. He did not beg. But he did talk. He was harmless, but not pleasant company. For one thing he smelled. Wine breath mixed with urine and strong body odor. Frank had a habit of approaching people and, leaning his face close to that of the target, he would ask questions. "Do you know the difference between a dangling participle and a split infinitive?" Frank would say. Most people pulled a scarf over their nose and rushed by, but the odd one would answer in the negative.

Frank never tried to educate. He would just shrug his shoulders and say most people didn't know the difference, as though this were one of the great ominous signs of the decline of western civilization. Senior townspeople claimed that Frank had had hardworking immigrant parents who provided him with a reasonable education and from whom, on the death of the father, Frank had received a small legacy, which he was determined to spend entirely on cheap wine. He could not see the point of squandering money on such unnecessary commodities as accommodation and clothes.

Undoubtedly there were times when Frank was both awake and sober, but no townsperson could ever recall seeing him in both these states at any one time. Two mysteries surrounded Frank's life. No one knew exactly where he lived or where he got his booze, presumably wine. Rumor had it that Frank had a shack out by the Etobicoke River about a half hour's walk from downtown. There is no record to indicate that anyone ever actually saw the shack but it was believed by most townspeople that the shack was out there somewhere. A minority believed that the shack didn't exist. They found it hard to believe that Frank could stay upright for a half hour at a time, never mind spend it walking from the shack to downtown.

If the shack existed, Frank didn't spend much time in it. He often slept overnight on the steps of the Bank of Commerce at the corner of Delby and Wellington Streets. He chose this because it was sufficiently off-center from the heart of Tupperton to allow the police to ignore him. Colder nights he would pass in any empty railroad open boxcar that happened to be in town. Frank wore a fedora and a long tweed great coat in the winter that he shed to reveal a woolen knit sweater and black pants with a piece of rope as a belt in the summer time. No matter how warm the summer day, Frank did not abandon the woolen sweater. This did little to enhance his odor.

Jacob Von Goerton could not have been more different from Frank. Jacob came from one of the town's prominent families. His father had been born in The Netherlands and had come to Canada as a teenager. Upon arriving in Canada, Horst got a job as a carpenter's apprentice and over the years had established a local reputation as a quality builder. Jacob had been on his pay role since leaving school at sixteen although he was absent from work more often than he was present. Jacob did not have the knack for carpentry and construction that was part of the very fiber of his father's being. Horst couldn't understand this and his disappointment was painfully obvious to the boy. Jacob's mother ran a perfect household but believed that outward expressions of endearments were improper and so demonstrated little affection for her son. Jacob kept himself reasonably clean and neat and, as far as anyone could discern, bathed regularly. While Frank was harmless and even friendly, Jacob could become volatile and vicious, traits that cost him his life before he reached his thirty-fourth birthday.

The one thing that Jacob had in common with Frank was the love of cheap booze. Jacob's father provided him with a home and the necessities of life, but limited his access to cash because he knew that Jacob would spend it on drink. Drink was what attracted Jacob to Frank. Frank always had some and both of them always wanted some. Although Jacob tried to avoid being seen in public with Frank, they were occasionally found arguing vehemently over some real or imagined slight and everyone assumed that somehow alcohol, or the lack of it, was the real topic of conversation. It is not really accurate to call their discussion an argument nor, for that matter, a discussion. Jacob would exhort or lament while Frank would listen with an inane smile.

Frank almost never went to church. I could say he never went except I have one very clear remembrance of his attendance at midnight Mass one Christmas eve. I had arrived at the tiny church just before midnight to find it packed with worshippers. The structure was so small that, even though there were not many Catholic families in the area, it was strained to capacity when they all attended special services such as at Easter or Christmas. I was thirteen and knew that my parents were in there somewhere but I couldn't make my way to them. I thought this might be a good excuse to skip out, but my dad would question me on the gist of the sermon and I'd better have the right answers.

Besides, where would a thirteen year old go at midnight on a cold Christmas Eve? I barely made it in the door when I was confronted by a wall of people forced to stand in the small alcove. I could hear the priest but see nothing. Shortly after I arrived, the door burst open behind me and in rushed Frank Donahue. I didn't have to turn around to know it was Frank. All the accompanying odors wafted relentlessly over my right shoulder, magnified by Frank's heavy breathing. I had no idea that Frank was so devout as to rush to Mass.

The door opened again and again the cold night air came in this time with Jacob Von Goerton. I didn't know it was Jacob until he started to issue threats to Frank.

"You slimy cocksucker!" Jacob said just above a whisper. "You think you can run in here and hide! Well, you got to come out when the Mass is over and I'll be waiting for you. You're dead you, fucking prick!" Jacob said this as he made the sign of the cross.

Meanwhile, Father Coughlin was sermonizing about the visitor who had arrived this day in our midst to bring a message of peace and good will to all mankind. The irony was lost on Jacob. At the end of the Mass, Frank managed to escape Jacob's wrath by slipping out with the crowd while Jacob had fallen asleep on the church steps.

It's fifteen years later and I have just found this story in an old notebook lost at the bottom of a desk drawer. I suppose the story is cute enough to let the public in on it but it occurs to me that perhaps people would like to know what happened to the characters mentioned in it.

Frank's body was found below the railway bridge that spanned the river near the town's center. The bridge had a concrete support structure that leveled into a platform meant to hold any equipment used in railway repairs. In practice it was almost never used for this purpose but was considered a great spot for kids to smoke and tell dirty jokes without fear of adult interruption. It was also a safe place to openly consume alcohol, which was prohibited either for sale or consumption anywhere outside a private residence in the town. Some say that Jacob and Frank met up there to share their booze and that the usual argument ensued followed by Frank being pushed or stumbling off the structure to the stepping stones that provided access across the river. His head was severely crushed on contact with the stone.

Very little follow-up was demanded of the police. Frank was expendable. Jacob disavowed any knowledge of the event. Case closed.

Jacob became even more devoted to booze after Frank's death. He also became more abusive of his wife, Annie and his three children. He came home one night, well fortified with alcohol and as soon as Annie said, "I've been worried sick," he hit her with the back of his hand. She stumbled backwards onto the floor.

Within seconds, Derek, their fourteen-year-old son, came downstairs from his bedroom. In one swipe grabbed a tennis trophy off the living room shelf and struck his father on the back of his head. The blow did not kill Jacob, but it did cause him to throw up and subsequently choke in his own vomit as he lay writhing on the living room floor. His wife and four children watched, unsure how much of the writhing was anger and how much was drink induced. Derek was actually charged with manslaughter, but was found not guilty.

Subway

By Catherine Astolfo

This first time I remember feeling that way was at the funeral, among the potted plants, when one aunt whispered to another, "I don't think she's been taught how to act properly at these functions." I had stood rebuffed, fingering my dress, a cactus amid the spray-painted blossoms. The fantasy occurred to me that I was from another planet, that I did not truly belong. That would explain this feeling of being lost and lonely, foreign, even when surrounded by family. Worse, I felt that I had let my father down, being accused of improper conduct at his funeral.

My fingers are trailing up and down my coat this time, but there are no whispered comments. In fact, it is the silence that threatens to conjure up that feeling again, this awkwardness. I sit among the chic Toronto business girls, a typical country cousin, my coat drab in comparison, my slacks trailing unstylishly over my boots. No one really looks at me, or points. If they do look in my direction, they seem to look right through me. This should make me feel better, but it doesn't.

I remember I tried to explain the feeling to Alex once. "You know what I mean?" I asked, begging understanding. "I feel like I don't belong, like something's wrong. Sort of ... the feeling you get when you're homesick."

Alex yawned, his huge mouth caverning in my face. "How can you be homesick when you're home?" We stared at each other, unable to bridge the gap in our thinking. "Let's go to bed," was his proposal, his solution to all thoughts of not belonging.

Holding Jacob in my arms in the hospital, I had thought that now the feeling would never return. This little round, perfect face looked up to me, depended upon me, and I was his wise and capable mother. It was not until I got him home, and could not quiet his painful screams, that I became overwhelmed by thoughts of being in the wrong place. When the pediatrician gave him something for colic, and he began to sleep through the night, I still could not shake the homesick feeling. There was something wrong about my being here with a baby, perhaps a computer error in heaven. Alex gave up trying to help.

"Relax, Cheryl," he would say. "Let me take the baby. You go shopping for the day."

But the fluorescent lights seemed to daze me, I could not think, I was unable to remember what I had thought about buying. So I trundled home again, sick and unhappy, greeted by Alex's anger.

"You are not trying," he flung at me. "You've got everything - a beautiful baby, a nice house, a husband who loves you - what do you want?"

My reply, "I want to feel that I belong," became a physical barrier between us, and Alex and I were never close again.

I wonder now, as I watch the distance hurl by through the windows of the train, whether that marriage might have worked, had I been willing to try a little harder. God knows I tried hard with David. I can picture Jacob and myself, wrapped in winter coats, stepping off the bus in Georgetown.

My mother was there, a pained expression coming over her face when she saw us.

"How could you leave him?" she demanded, kissing Jacob hello. "All alone out there in that god-forsaken prairie town! What went wrong? You were so happy..."

I lit a cigarette as soon as we got to her car.

"When did you take that up? You never smoked before. I hate to see you doing this."

Again the feeling hit me, achingly, filling me. I felt that I could hardly breathe from the pressure. "Mother," I told her, my voice strong and sure. "I'm a grown woman now. I know what I'm doing."

I had told myself that what I needed was to become established in my own place, with Jacob, and to take up my nursing career again. Then, I told myself, the homesick feeling would never return - I would belong.

A group of teen-age girls race onto the train, flushed and excited, giggling loudly. They are playing "chicken", racing from one car to the next, trying to do it before the doors close. They are very noisy and inconsiderate of others attempting to board the train; people look at them with contempt. But I feel like smiling. I remember the days of not caring, of thinking only of myself and the fun of the moment. Those times don't last, girls, I tell them silently; enjoy them while you may. When had it happened, I wonder? When had I become a sad and cynical, middle-aged woman? It seems such a short time ago, yet eons, that I was the same age as Noreen is now.

Noreen. She is everything I always wanted to be. Beautiful, confident, intelligent. It pleases me to think that I might have had something to do with her success as a person. She is so well adjusted to this world. Strange that she is the child of someone as confused as I. Stranger still that she was born of the union between David and myself.

I met him at a party. As usual, I was sitting in a corner talking to my girlfriend, pretending to have a good time, consuming enough gin to make myself believe it, too. Mainly I was thinking of Jacob, wondering if I had been out too much lately, mystified by his tantrums and anger. "Two-year-olds are like that," my mother assured me, but I did not fully believe her. Always with Jacob I felt not quite adequate for the job.

The man in the bright blue shirt had obviously caught everyone's attention, especially mine. It had been a long time since a man had attracted me, but this one was extraordinary. Tall, lean, dark ... he glided around the room, dancing energetically with different girls, listening with intensity to every word each person spoke to him.

To his question, "Do you dance?" I answered flippantly, "I do, but I don't want to just now", my heart beating fiercely, my face flushed and afraid. I kept room-distance away from him all evening, yet I was aware of his every move.

When it happened that our cars were parked alongside one another, and when he trailed after me out the door, I felt trapped. I panted like a frightened mouse.

"I didn't get your name," he said, his face close to mine, his voice curious.

"Cheryl," I mumbled, feeling transported back to Grade 5 when my first love interest had actually turned to look at me, and I had become aware that my nose was running.

"Would you like to go to the Donut shop for a coffee, Cheryl?" He held the door of his car invitingly.

Seated on stools, drinking coffee and eating chocolate éclairs, we exchanged light conversation; he lit my cigarettes and told me things to make me smile. I felt strangely unfamiliar again, as though I were watching myself on a television screen. I knew I had hungered for some male companionship, but I could not allow myself to be drawn into his dark eyes.

He asked for my phone number, but he did not call. I threw myself into caring for Jacob, paying more attention to him than ever before. We sat for hours playing his little games, talking, looking at picture books. Oddly, his behaviour seemed to be unchanged; perhaps my mother had been right after all. I relaxed a little. I taught him to say, "Hello," when he picked up the telephone (it was always my mother who called, and she was thrilled to hear his little voice).

I was doing the dishes the first time David called, and Jacob answered the telephone. There was silence for a moment, so I came out to the living room and took the receiver from him.

"Is this Cheryl?"

"Yes, it is."

"Oh. This is David. I met you at Linda's party. I...thought I had the wrong number."

"No, that was my little boy Jacob." Silence. "I'm divorced." I drew in my breath, hating him and myself for having to explain.

But it seemed to make no difference to David. In fact, I found myself inviting him to dinner, found his acceptance lively and enthusiastic. I think now that perhaps he thought I was safe, that I would not want to think of marrying him.

David and Jacob became instant friends. They rolled on the living-room rug, played dead, "shot" each other from behind the couch, tickled themselves into gales of laughter. I stood apart from them, unable to be so free, so uninhibited. Yet I knew I should enjoy this, be glad for Jacob, whose only male contact was a once-a-year trip to the prairies. David was good with Jacob, patient and firm, something I could never achieve. Later, when the baby was in bed, we lounged in front of the stereo (my $100 special), talking in soft tones.

David lay sprawled beside me, natural and comfortable, whereas I, in my own living room, felt like a visitor.

"Have you been alone long?"

"Nearly a year." I smiled into my glass of wine. "It's funny, you know, but I could have said that I've been alone for a long, long time and both answers would be just as truthful."

We looked at one another carefully, and then he kissed me. It was a long, slow, gentle kiss, the kind that thrilled through my entire body. Years later he told me that he had felt sorry for me, and so had kissed me, but at the time it had seemed to be the night, the closeness, the attraction between us.

"Do you want to make love?" he asked.

I remember the wonder that I felt at his words. No one had ever asked me before, least of all Alex. It had always been assumed that I would want to, that I would not be able to resist his masculine charm. The memory of that first time with David is still vivid - the smoothness of him, the gentleness of his touch, the softness of his hair. God, how I long for him. However he made me feel about him, I could still make love with him, drive him to ecstasy, have him bring me to orgasm.

It seems silly now, but it was after the lovemaking that I suffered.

"What if Jacob wakes up and finds you here?" I whispered to David frantically in the middle of the night.

"Relax, Cheryl. He's only a baby. He'll just be glad to see me, that's all."

Relax, Cheryl. This I was constantly being told. David's repetition of Alex's words were frightening, an omen. I kept quiet the rest of the night, my guilt a thundering in my chest.

And of course David was right. When Jacob hopped out of his crib and jumped on the bed with his usual glorious, "Mama!" he turned with delight to "Vud", who responded with hugs and tumbles. "Vud" soon became "Bud", something Jacob has never let die.

I stare at the floor of the train, embarrassed. Crying on a subway is definitely not done in Toronto. Faces must be stoic, less than human. Emotions should not be floating on the surface, where everyone can see. But the sadness in me is a thing beyond my control, something with a life of its own. The pictures inside my head seem so real, so vivid, and I wonder at their loss. I feel more a part of them now than I did at the time.

Those days with David were mostly happy, and Jacob and I took pleasure in his presence. There were days of picnics, the zoo, a show, puttering around the apartment, walking through the park. And there were the nights ... long, slow, enjoyable nights ... that led to romping mornings with Jacob. For much of the time, I told myself that my happiness stemmed from Jacob's pleasure. But that gradually became untrue, and I realized that I must feel deeply for David.

"I love you," I whispered against his shoulder one night, my words loud in the darkness. I could not see his face, but I could feel his body stiffen.

"Do me a favour, Cheryl," he said, his voice cold. "Don't ever do that ... don't ever love me."

He stayed away for a week. Jacob and I wandered sadly through the days, each feeling neglected and abandoned. When David appeared at the door one night, flowers in hand, I took his presence as a confession that he could not stay away from us, that in his own way, he loved us, too. But I did not mention the word again.

Over the next year, he often left us for days at a time. Then he would always reappear, loving and happy, twice as affectionate, and I began to take his absences as the need for his own space. I did not think that he had anyone else.

He took me to parties and dances. To all of his friends he said, "This is my best girl - Cheryl", but I always spent the time alone, while he danced with other women. Somehow I managed to make excuses, telling myself that I didn't like to dance anyway, smiling through everything. I was frightened of losing him, of breaking the tenuous hold I had on him. We never quarreled, for I never disagreed with him: never asked anything of him that he was not willing to give. Whereas with Alex I had struggled to make everything equal between us (or so I thought), I never demanded a thing from David. Until that day in February.

The train lurches to a stop and I grab the pole in front of my seat. People rush off to the platform or shoulder their way into the car. A huge woman dressed in black and smelling of fish squeezes into the seat next to me. I turn my head to the window, catching my reflection in the glass. My hair is nicely curled around my face, the way Octavio had meant it to be, but somehow the style seems old-fashioned in comparison to most of the women on the subway. My face is lined and pale, looking every bit my fifty-one years. Even my eyes, once alive and blue, seem dulled with age. My friends still tell me that I look much younger, but I think they are just being kind.

The memory of the look in his eyes that winter day still makes me shudder.

"You've done this on purpose, haven't you?" His voice was raised, almost a scream, and his face was purple with rage.

"No, David, no... please..." The tears almost choked my speech.

"Well, what the hell are you doing here, telling me this? What am I supposed to do about it?" He flung himself to the floor and paced, a caged animal, his hands gesturing in the air. "I'm not tied to you ... I'm not obliged to do a thing about this. It's your fault, your mistake." He turned threateningly. "How do I even know it's mine?"

I slumped back on his couch, struggling to breathe normally, watching the room swim before me. I thought, I must not put up with this, but I could not move. I felt dependent, chained to him, forced to bear his anger. Something told me that I was punishable, that I deserved this beating of words.

"What do you intend to do? I hope you don't expect me to marry you, just because you're pregnant. For God's sake, don't you know anything about contraception? I thought you had one of those diaphragms."

"I do, but the doctor said ... they're not ... fool proof..."

"Fool is right," he hissed. "Dammit, how did you get me into this? I only felt sorry for you, living alone with a child. I should have known better." He hammered the wall with his fist, each blow driving into my skull.

My legs unsteady, I groped my way to the bathroom and vomited violently. I spent the night in his bed, sick and frightened, while he slept on the couch. It was not quite morning when he came to see me, his shoulders slumped, tears streaked on his face.

"I'm sorry, Cheryl," he whispered, his voice broken. "It's just that ... I can't get married. I'm too frightened of it. And I don't know if I've ever been in love with anyone, including you. I just ... can't."

I put my hand gently on his head. "It's all right, David. Just move in with Jacob and me until I'm well again. Please. And then you can leave."

He nodded, collapsing in my arms, a boy in a man's body.

My mother was appalled. "My God, Cheryl! How can you do this to me? First the divorce, now this - how will I ever tell the family, or face the neighbours?"

"I won't come home often, Mother. I promise. I'm not feeling well anyway."

But she was with me as much as she could be, taking care of Jacob, making me tea. For I was terribly sick. I lost weight rather than gaining it, as I could keep nothing in my stomach. Finally the doctor put me in the hospital to wait for the last month. Through a semi-conscious daze, full of dreams and disbelief, I was aware of David, hovering, but not too closely. I barely remembered the delivery of the baby, or the days that followed. Unlike the birth of Jacob, this one was plagued with uncertainty and unhappiness.

A full week after the baby had been born, I awoke to find David sitting by my bedside, head in hands. I touched his elbow and he jumped.

"Cheryl!" The relief in his eyes was almost more than I could bear. "My God, I'm so glad to see you awake. I was so afraid."

I tried to speak, but no sound came. Weakness drained me.

"It's all right, darling. I'm so sorry this happened." He held my hand tightly, his face sincere, his words rehearsed. "We're going to get married. As soon as you're well enough. I didn't realize how much I loved you until now."

I smiled faintly, wanting to believe him, needing to believe him. "The baby...?" I whispered, tense.

"He's fine. He's a little small, only five pounds, but he's strong." This time David's voice was pure and proud. "How's John David Mahoney for a name?" At my nod, he smiled. "I'm so glad you like it. Get well, sweetheart." His soft kiss on my lips kept my sleep peaceful.

An old lady gets on the train, her gait plodding and tight, her face pinched with the pain of age. I cannot stop staring at her. I picture myself, twenty years from now, riding the subway. I am unable to imagine it. Instead, I think of myself at home, plump and red-faced, sitting by a window, watching my grandchildren play. Or perhaps I will be slim and smart, my grey hair graceful, my age a secret. I don't know. I only know that sometimes I feel very, very old already, and that perhaps this is a bad sign.

The years I spent with David seem a curiosity to me now. I wonder how I could have passed through so much time without taking any active part at all.

Instead there seemed to be a flow of children, diapers, coffee with the neighbours, dinners spoiled because David didn't come home, aches and pains and spats that had to solved for the boys, runny noses, broken shoelaces ... and I? Where was I this whole time? No longer Cheryl - just "Mummy" or "the Wife", or the lady who lived in the yellow house on the corner. David and I made love often, but we did not love. For him, it was a marriage of conscience; for me, a bond of gratitude. I felt tied to him, grateful to him, for staying with me and for caring for the children and me.

Instinctively I knew that he was never faithful to me, and the pitying looks that neighbours often gave me cemented the suspicion. But I did not seem to begrudge him the affairs. We never talked to one another long enough to disagree. In four years, I bore four babies, giving us five little children to care for. David delighted in them all, especially Noreen, our only little girl, our last.

"You won't be having any more babies, Cheryl," Dr. Reynolds told me. "I'll have to cauterize the tubes. You've become thinner and sicker with each child; the next one could be your undoing. David thinks it's a good idea."

And I did too, I guess, though my emotions were too deadened to know. I watched myself caring for the children, hugging them, playing with them, tending their physical needs; detached, foreign, strange. I often thought of my father's funeral, of the fact that I had laughed during the service. So with my children I tried to be perfect, following all the aunts' advice, listening to my mother's every word.

If their childhood was difficult, they do not show it. Perhaps it was difficult only for me. Now that they have grown up, we are good friends, and they tell me they love me. They seem to be decent, ordinary citizens, capable of loving and understanding, and I think they are kind to their own children. The boys hold regular jobs, have nicely pretty wives, and live in homes something like the one we lived in with David.

And then there is Noreen. I consider my daughter spectacular, someone I am in awe of and perhaps envy. This may be because she has stayed with me through everything, and still shares my life. She is not married because she does not want to be, not yet. She has a career and she loves to travel. She is lovely, confident, at peace with herself and the world. She lives everything fully, dives into every activity with all her strength and concentration. She is the person I always wanted to be. In recent months it is as if our roles have reversed, and she has taken to mothering me.

"You can do it," she said to me this morning. "You are very attractive, and intelligent, and you know this job well. Now go out there and get it!"

My nursing career was one of the constants in my life with David and the children. Every Saturday I worked at the hospital. When the children were older, I attended lectures, volunteered my services. The only books I read were medical, and I kept up-to-date with every new technique. I was often in demand with the doctors.

"Mrs. Mahoney, would you look in on Mr. King in the morning? I'd really like your opinion on his progress week to week."

One of my best assets was the ability to be calm and cool in an emergency. I was always able to remain detached. Death and illness never seemed to bother me; I accepted them as I accepted everything else.

Noreen was eighteen years old, just entering college, and the boys had moved away from home, when the cocoon in which I had wrapped myself began to fall apart.

"Cheryl, I want to talk to you."

David sat me in the living room and began his usual pacing, hands waving in the air for emphasis.

"We've been together twenty-two years. In most of that time, I don't think either of us has been happy."

At my gesture, he cautioned me not to interrupt. I think his speech was too well rehearsed to bear interruptions.

"I've fallen in love, Cheryl, maybe for the first time. She's my secretary and she's been with me for five years. It just shows how out of touch we are with one another, for you've never even met her." He paused and then sat beside me on the couch. "The children are grown now, so there's no problem. I'm sure Noreen will want to stay with you. She knows about Margaret, and she understands. I think we should sell the house. I'll give you all the money from the sale, as long as you don't ask for alimony. That's a big enough sum to get you through many years."

I stared at him, stunned, silent. Once more the old feeling returned, the homesickness, the floating in unreality.

"Don't look at me like that, Cheryl," he said softly, patronizingly, patting my hand. "You can't have been happy either. What has our relationship done for you? You're forty-eight years old and you've been nowhere, done nothing. Now you have a chance to live again."

Been nowhere? Done nothing? Was this house nowhere? Was raising five children nothing? Was he right?

I went to look at her once. I made certain that she did not see me, afraid she may have seen a picture of me. She was about twenty-eight, slim, beautiful, vivacious. Her smile was lovely, her manner interesting and lively. From the television screen of my mind I watched my life unravel.

At first I balked at selling the house. This was where my babies were born, I told myself. How can I leave it? Then I realized that Noreen was right. "There are too many memories here, Mom. Let's get a new place, where we can look forward instead of backward. A snazzy apartment, maybe."

So we began to look - and I had fun doing it. It was pleasant to find what I wanted, to take no one else's opinion into account. Even Noreen refused to judge. "I won't be there as long as you will, Mom. I'll only be home on week-ends while I'm in college, and after that, who knows?" I found an apartment building close to the city and I decorated it with new things. The only articles I kept from my life with David were clothes and pictures.

The memories of David leaving, of selling the house and moving into the apartment, of the divorce and his subsequent marriage, were devoid of tears. It wasn't until those days and months that followed, that I saw myself reach out and begin to feel again. My God, it was painful. I spent so many nights alone, crying into the darkness, aching for his touch. I passed so many hours in a daze of fear and loneliness, gazing into a future that seemed bleak and frightening. I cursed Margaret's name a thousand times, resentful of her youth, feeling old and cast aside. But when it was over, I could see again, feel again.

The homesickness left me whenever I turned the key in my apartment door. I began to take pleasure in little things; watching what I liked on television, lounging in the nude, spending hours in the tub. I had suddenly, after all these years, discovered my likes, my dislikes, my opinions, my desires.

When Noreen came home on weekends, and in later years when she went out to work, we talked and laughed together. It was she who brought up the subject of a job.

"Why don't you go out to work, Mom? I know you don't really need the money, but it could make a big change in your life."

"What would I do, though? I don't really want to go back to the hospital."

"Well, I just happened to see this ad in the paper." She spread the want ads out on the floor. "They would like a registered nurse to be in charge of drug administration, educating people about new drugs available, making sure medicines are properly used. It sounds interesting, different."

Sending out the resumé was not difficult.

It is the interview that frightens me. The subway train lurches to a stop and I trail out with all the other people. I get a little lost finding the right building, but suddenly I am there, right on time.

The woman is my age, kind, soft spoken. She starts out with the usual questions, then stops. "Mrs. Mahoney, is there something bothering you?"

I surprise myself by blurting, "I'm very nervous. I'm coming back into the work force after twenty-five years and although I know I can do the job, I'm just out of practice convincing someone else that I can."

We spend the rest of the interview in a coffee shop, comfortable, relaxed, talking as if we've known each other for years. She tells me that she wants me for the position, that I am the best qualified, and have the manner and outlook that she thinks will suit the job perfectly. We shake hands, fill out papers, and I meet the rest of the staff.

And now here I am, back riding the subway. My reflection looks at little better this time, less strained, less tired. I cannot wait to tell Noreen. I will treat her to a steak dinner.

Soon, I know, I will feel a part of this crowd. I am certain that I will teach myself to dress as well as the other women do. I must learn to give myself time, not to expect perfection. I do know that I am good at my trade, that I will do the job well.

I arrive back at my home stop, so I stand and try to look dignified. I have come a long way, not in distance, not in time, but in learning. I can feel so deeply now that I even cry on subways. My longing for David will pass; perhaps I will find someone else to fill the sexual yearning. I do belong to my apartment, to my children, my grandchildren, and now to my job. But most of all, to myself.

Although I may feel the homesickness, the strangeness, threaten from time to time, I think I will always be able to reach out and steady myself, as I do now with the subway pole. It has taken me over fifty years to do so.

I walk out through the doors of the train and head for the stairs. A man who is sweeping the floor whistles at me and I feel giddy. "Imagine, at my age!" I will tell Noreen, very proper and insulted, but she will know how flattered and pleased I am.

I walk out into the sunshine, into the bustle and noise of this city world, out of the darkness of the subway tunnel.

No Further Action

By Tom Sullivan

Eddy stood at attention, shoulders sagged and right finger and thumb nervously massaging his left hand's index finger. The vice-principal's office was intended to impress and intimidate and remained consistent with the hundred and twenty-year-old structure that formed the main building of Mount St. Elburn College. The floors and desk and walls were all of solid wood and lent an air of authority and respectability that seemed built into the very fabric of the prestigious school. Brother Alfred stood behind the dark mahogany desk. Dark walnut book cases lined the walls and were filled with leather and cloth-bound volumes, most of which had not been touched, other than to be dusted, for years. A large Formica-topped beige table sat incongruously within three feet of the vice-principal's desk and was overlain with folders and stacks of papers. The desk itself was bare except for a pad of paper, a pen and a telephone placed well to the corner, a necessary concession to modernity.

"You do realize, Edward, that if we do not have names of other students involved, you must bear full responsibility for the embarrassment that this incident has brought to Mount St. Elburn's." said Brother Alfred, glancing alternatively at Eddy and the blank pad of paper on his desk. Eddy spoke softly but firmly: "I don't really know who the other boys were, Brother Alfred. They were getting out of the pool just as I jumped in."

"You could identify the boys in the school year book."

"No, I don't think so," replied Eddy.

"Very well….prepare." Brother Alfred walked slowly across the office floor to one of the floor-to-ceiling cabinets and took out a long thin reed-like wooden switch. He returned to the desk and laid the switch across the desk in front of Eddy. "Edward, I will offer you one last opportunity to reconsider your response: who are the other boys involved?"

In reply, Eddy put his hands on the Brother's desk, leaned forward, closed his eyes and gently shook his head and whispered, "I don't know.."

The act of leaning with both hands on the desk was not one of defiance, but of submission. This was the position one assumed when told to "prepare." Eddy kept his eyes closed to await the blow. It came swiftly and strongly. Even in the 1950's this punishment was considered by many to be barbaric and would have been unthinkable in the public school system. But at St. Elburn's it was still tolerated. The board of directors had debated at length over the issue of "the cane" as it was called and in the end, decided to keep it. It was considered part of the tradition of the school and appealed to parents who wanted their boys raised in a "stern but loving Christian environment": an environment which they were unwilling to or incapable of providing at home. The board members emphasized in their report that the cane be used only in extreme circumstances and that should more than one blow of the cane be administered, the offending boy's parents were to be notified and given the option of being present.

Eddy's crime, which put the school's image in jeopardy, was considered serious enough to warrant one stroke of the cane.

Earlier that afternoon, Eddy had been following four older boys as they crossed the open campus. On the terrace, some hundred and fifty yards away were visiting dignitaries who were on campus as guests of the school principal, Brother Norton. These were school benefactors and the principal felt that a favorable impression was essential. The older boys, sensing an opportunity to create a bit of mayhem, stripped off their clothes and dove naked into the school's outdoor pool.

As the last one dove in, he turned quickly to Eddy and shouted, "Come on, stupid." Being included in an activity, even a stupid one, with senior boys, was something few frosh could resist. Eddy's almost automatic response was to strip off his clothes and dive in. Eddy swam the length of the pool and clambered out the other side. The senior boys dove in, did a quick u-turn and climbed out the same end of the pool that they dove into. This meant that Eddy was on the opposite end of the pool from his clothes whereas the senior boys seemed to emerge from the pool, grab their clothes and be gone almost in one motion.

Eddy ran naked down the concrete apron of the pool, grabbed his clothes and headed for the trees, but not before he had a clear view of his math teacher, Mr. Handleton hurrying toward the pool area... and Mr. Handleton had a clear view of a naked Eddy running toward the small copse of trees to pull on his clothes. Eddy made his way to his room in the dorm, but no sooner arrived there than he was notified that he was expected immediately in the vice-principal's office.

Eddy now lay on his bed staring unfocused into the darkness that surrounded him. The punishment had been swift and painful... one quick whack of the cane across his rear-end. At one time this would have been administered to the bare behind but the moderate board members felt that this was too degrading. The thought of the experience seemed to beckon up a burning sensation and Eddy turned on his side and wrapped the pillow around his head. The pain wasn't severe now... actually it subsided very quickly after the blow was dealt. He had braced himself to receive the assault determined not to show any reaction at all, and yet, when the blow came, he had burst into uncontrollable tears. He had felt moisture flood his nose and a scream burst from his chest as his resolve exploded. When he first returned to his room he could not control his feelings. His eyes ached from crying and fluids built in his nose and throat. He held his breath and tried not to swallow or cry. But he could hold out only briefly and then he would let out a gasp and his whole body would shake.

He lay on his back in the darkness and the tender buttock seemed swollen and alternately hot and cold. He wiped his nose and his sweaty face on the sheet and tried to relax. Pain had given way to anger and a sense of humiliation. He was angry with himself partly because he had been so easily duped into participating in the foolish prank but mostly he was angry because he had cried instantaneously. He was dismissed from the office immediately after the blow and was seen by other students sobbing as he ran. He felt that he would face ridicule as long as he remained at St. Elburn's.

At the time, the boys had bowed their heads and turned toward their lockers in silence with just a trace of a smile and a surreptitious glance at their neighbors. But Eddy was sure that they had formed a lasting opinion...

Eddy Duncan could not take punishment. From that point on, he would be a suck, a sissy. He was angry at his own weakness. Eventually, the anger subsided, the crying stopped and drowsiness overtook him. He was gently drifting into sleep.

Eddy was aware of his door opening. This could not be Albert, his roommate, who had just left two days ago to spend time with visiting relatives in his hometown. Maybe it's some of the boys coming to ridicule the sissy. Eddy did not respond... he hoped that the intruder would believe that he was asleep and leave as quietly as he entered. A figure quietly crossed the floor, pulled Eddy's desk chair up beside the bed and sat quietly for a few seconds.

The figure reached out and gently stroked Eddy's forehead. The figure whispered: "You've had quite a day, Eddy. I want you to know that I think you were very brave. You took punishment rather than tell on the others. That's what our Lord did. He took punishment for the sins of others."

From the first words Eddy knew the voice. Brother Bernard was a gentle, kindly man who always made himself available for students for extra help in Latin. Eddy felt himself relax as Brother Bernard gently stroked his head and his cheeks and talked reassuringly. Eddy remained silent and still, but became increasingly aware of the physical contact. His skin seemed ultra sensitive and alert. Eddy felt drowsy yet aroused. His chest tightened and a bead of sweat formed on his upper lip. And, for some reason that he could not identify, he got an erection.

At first he was not even aware. It was as though his body and penis were one and the same and the stroking action of Brother Bernard's hand on his forehead and cheeks was a form of masturbation. Eddy felt a sharp sense of shame. Brother Bernard had come to his room to offer him comfort and kind words and he had responded sexually. Brother Bernard lightly massaged Eddy's chest and encouraged him to relax and get some sleep.

As Bernard drew his hand away, he brushed ever so lightly against Eddy's erect penis. Brother Bernard paused and then put his thumb and forefinger around the shaft of Eddy's penis and whispered: "My, what have we here?" His voice was quiet and still gently soothing.

The next day was Tuesday, and the school was on a "day B", which meant that Eddy had Latin, taught by Brother Bernard in period two. Eddy entered the class behind a small knot of boys and tried to remain as unobtrusive as possible. He kept his head down and sat quickly in his assigned seat. During the class, he glanced periodically at Brother Bernard expecting some small conspiratorial sign: a nod, a quick smile... but Brother Bernard gave no sign of recognition other than to ask Eddy in turn to conjugate the verb video, which Eddy did accurately and perfunctorily. Eddy spent the latter half of the class analyzing the situation and trying to detect some message in Bernard's behavior. But Bernard always was a man hard to read. He was quiet, seldom raising his voice unnecessarily. In his efficient way he made Latin interesting and interspersed his grammatical structures and synthesis with stories of ancient Rome, which the students enjoyed. Over the past few years, Latin enrolment had increased by about a third. This delighted the school's administration since in the 1950's, Latin was essential for boys entering the seminary, and every boy at St. Elburn's was encouraged to at least consider this option.

Eddy's school life slipped back into normalcy. Although he felt that his image had suffered because of his reaction to the discipline, there had been no taunting or snide derogatory remarks. Eddy had never seen another boy's response to the cane... perhaps his reaction had been more typical than he had expected. Perhaps other boys harbored fears that their reaction would be similar or perhaps worse if they were ever subjected to the same punishment.

Eddy wrote an article about the spirit and dedication of the school's junior basketball team for the school newspaper and he continued attending the astronomy club which was chaired by an unkempt chubby kid named Oscar who never seemed to do anything with any degree of efficiency but whose knowledge of astronomy seemed encyclopedic... at least to the other four members of the club.

One morning, when the day promised to be dull and boring both academically and atmospherically, Eddy was handed one of the four yellow notices that the class Brother distributed that day to boys in homeroom. It was the policy of the school that each of the boys pays a visit to the chaplain/guidance counselor at least once per term. These sessions were both academic and spiritual in nature and the boys were encouraged to discuss with Brother Charles any matter that was bothering them or any problem that they wished to discuss. Although the majority of the boys had no intention of revealing anything of their personal life, they often stretched the session to the limit with idle talk in order to avoid returning to class too quickly.

Any Sports topic often aided the delaying process since Brother Charles was an ardent fan. He was not really athletic himself, although he played a fair game of tennis, but he took a keen interest in all sports and considered it a vehicle by which he related to the boys. He was also very sympathetic to boys who complained of the teaching methods or idiosyncrasies of the various teachers.

Mr. Merriwell had an irritating habit of constantly clearing his throat while lecturing and Brother Henry's insistence on perfection in lab reports included the correct placement of dots over the letter "i." Students claimed that there were only two marks possible in Brother Henry's class, 100% and zero. Brother Charles listened to everyone's complaints quietly and calmly and had a way of making vices seemed like virtues.

"Brother Henry knows that you have great ability and he wants you to live up to your potential." Occasionally, it was possible to persuade Brother Charles to write a note to a teacher to get an extension on a project deadline, provided the student was able to deliver a convincing story of family dysfunction or illness. This day, Eddy was to report to Brother Charles at the beginning of period three.

Eddy felt quite relaxed and comfortable in discussion with Brother Charles. Surprisingly, Brother often offered boys a cigarette during the interview. He justified it by saying that it created a more relaxed, open atmosphere. Since smoking was officially discouraged and greatly restricted on campus, it lent a conspiratorial air to the meeting, which encouraged boys to take Brother Charles into their confidence. It also allowed Brother Charles to satisfy his nicotine craving. Many boys took the offered cigarette and some were initiated into a life-long addiction through Brother Charles' friendly gesture. Brother Charles always preferred that boys accepted the offer since he felt that somehow a refusal was a censure of his own smoking. Eddy politely refused.

Brother Charles always prepared well for each interview. He commented on Eddy's scholastic progress and asked how he was enjoying the astronomy club and congratulated Eddy on his school newspaper contribution... all this while barely referring to his notes. These interviews usually lasted about fifteen minutes and were almost always concluded shortly after Brother Charles was assured that all campus life was fine with the interviewee.

But when asked, Eddy blurted out the story of the incident with Brother Bernard. He had no idea that the incident had bothered him, but when asked if there was anything troubling him, the whole image of the sexual encountered flooded vividly to mind.

Brother Charles facial muscles relaxed and he visibly paled. He even paused in mid-puff. "This is a very serious accusation, Eddy." Charles' voice was barely above a whisper.

This response surprised Eddy. He didn't think of it as an accusation at all. From his perspective, Brother Bernard was almost an innocent bystander, and Eddy had hoped since the incident that he had chosen to forget Eddy's indiscretion. Eddy found himself defending Brother Bernard and assuming full responsibility. After all, he had not been forced into any situation and he had become aroused well before Bernard had made any sexual contact.

Brother Charles admonished Eddy to keep the matter strictly to himself. "We don't want you to get a bad reputation here at the school, Edward," Brother Charles said. "We understand that young men your age are very sensitive and have to guard against impurity at all times. At the time, you had just undergone quite a traumatic punishment and were understandably not in full control. Do your best to put the incident behind you and

I'm sure that Brother Bernard will be willing to forgive and forget." With this, Eddy was given the permission slip that would readmit him to class.

Next morning, Eddy received a further slip, on plain white paper, asking him to attend a meeting in the principal's office immediately before lunch. Usually, a class-hours summons to the principal's office meant something quite serious, such as a death in the family or expulsion from school. It was also normal practice to spend a lengthy time on the hard office bench before being admitted into Brother Norton's office, and while keeping the student waiting was a matter of course, no student ever arrived late for an appointment with the principal. However, Eddy was kept waiting less than a minute.

As the secretary, Miss Hazelette, emerged from the principal's office, she gave Eddy a brief look and a nod and Eddy slipped quietly inside while the door was being held open for him. Miss Hazelette then went out and closed the door behind her. In the office were Brother Norton, standing behind and to the right of his desk and Brothers Bernard and Charles each flanking the desk in a formation that resembled that of a welcoming committee. One look told Eddy that this was no welcoming committee.

Brother Norton looked serious, but somehow relaxed. Brother Charles seemed reluctant to look at Eddy, somewhat in the manner of a student who had just run to the principal to tattle on a naughty classmate. Brother Bernard was almost unrecognizable. His eyes bulged, his face was pale, and he was constantly licking his lips. This quiet, placid man seemed almost maniacal in appearance, although he so far had said nothing.

Brother Norton wasted no time. "Eddy, do you know why we are here?"

"Yes, Brother."

"This is a pretty serious allegation you are making."

For some reason Eddy replied, "I didn't mean to tell anyone."

"But, you already have told Brother Charles," responded Brother Norton, abruptly. "Who else have you told?"

"No one," said Eddy.

"Well," said Brother Norton, "I think that since you chose to tell Brother Charles, it is only fair that we hear Brother Bernard's side of the story."

Almost like a courtroom attorney, with head down and arms folded in from of him, Brother Norton spoke to Brother Bernard.

"Brother Bernard, would you tell us what happened?"

Eddy felt very uncomfortable. He didn't want to hear details and if, at that moment they had asked him to sign a hand written confession assuming all responsibility and agreeing to spend eternity in hell as a punishment, he felt that he would have done it as long as they would agree not to drag up all the details of that night.

Brother Bernard spoke in a furious outburst. "I went in to offer the boy comfort and solace and I stroked his head and the next thing I know this thing is glaring up at me. Well, I was shocked...so shocked that I don't precisely recall the subsequent turn of events, but I do know that I was just floored to find one of our boys so thoroughly and blatantly sexually aroused as a response to Christian comfort..."

Brother Bernard's eyes were ablaze and his voice almost a high feminine pitch. A little spittle formed in the corner of his mouth and he glared at Eddy, defying him to deny the facts as Bernard was stating them.

Eddy reflected on Brother Charles words. Of course he wouldn't tell anybody. He had never talked about sex with his parents. And he couldn't let his mother know that he had had any such experience. Eddy apologized sincerely to Brother Bernard and vowed that he would never tell a soul... not even his parents. Brother Bernard accepted the apology and Eddy was allowed to return to class with no further action to be taken on the matter.

Two years later, Brother Bernard was transferred as bursar to a mixed-sex day school. The job of Bursar had to do chiefly with the financial aspects of the school and involved minimal contact with students. After two years in this position, Brother Bernard left the school under undisclosed circumstances.

Thirty-two years later the school's board of trustees was instructed by the courts to compensate victims of sexual molestation in the sum of one million three hundred thousand dollars. Thirty-six former students were named as recipients of the compensation. Eddy was not one of them. He was one of the unacknowledged victims in this tragedy, along with the dozens of guiltless dedicated clerics who sacrificed so much to share their beliefs and their lives for the betterment of their students... and whose saintly lives have been smeared and denigrated because of the acts of a relative few.

The End